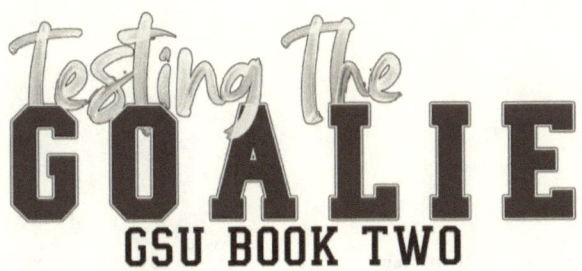

GSU BOOK TWO

LAURA JOHN

If you're one of those who like saying "yes, Daddy," this book is for you!

DEAR READER,

This is a M/M romance that features elements of DD/lb but has NO ABDL play. The kink is kept light but with the heat turned on high!

For a full list of content warnings, please proceed to my website: https://www.authorlaurajohn.com/testing-the-goalie

CHAPTER ONE

THE SUN BEATS down on my back, and the sand shifts beneath my feet. A permanent smile is on my face as I make my way back to the resort I'm staying at after a leisurely stroll.

I needed this change of scenery. Don't get me wrong, I love the cold and spending most of my time on ice, but sometimes, it's nice to get away, be myself, and not the goalie for Green Spring University's hockey team.

My feet carry me directly to my hotel's outdoor bar the second I'm on the property again. It's hot as balls already and a cold beer is exactly what I need right about now.

When I approach the area, my eyes immediately land on a tall drink of water of a man leaning against the bar. Running my tongue along my lips, I slow my pace and take in the sexy man. He has dark, thick hair and a jawline so fucking perfect it should be illegal. His eyes are covered by sunglasses, like my own, hiding what they actually look like, but I'm going to imagine they're captivating. His body is perfection—toned abs on display for all to see, well-defined arms, and thick thighs.

God bless the man who designed this guy's Speedo. It's leaving nothing to the imagination, but I'm not complaining.

With a steady pace, I head to the bar, stopping beside the sexy man and flagging down the bartender, who offers a smile. I order a beer, needing something to sip on while I try to get the stranger's attention.

"This your first time at this resort?" I ask the guy once I have my beer in hand, finally making him turn toward me.

He raises his sunglasses, resting them on top of his head, and damn, his eyes are so fucking blue they match the clear sky. It almost makes it hard to breathe for a moment.

A sexy smirk crosses his lips, and he stands tall, straightening his shoulders. His eyes slowly roam over my body, blatantly checking me out and causing a shiver of desire to ripple down my spine. "It is, what about you?"

"Same. I heard about this place from a friend and knew I had to visit. So far, it's been amazing."

The first thing I wanted to do once I finally got a break from college and hockey was get away from everything and everyone. So, the moment I could, I booked a trip for a week in the sun at an all-inclusive resort on an island far away from any of the usual hassles and stress. The resort is perfect because not only is there no technology allowed—no worries of videos being recorded—but it also caters to the gay community. The moment I discovered this place, I knew I wanted to be here.

"I'd definitely return here," he shares, leaning in a little closer with an ease I wish I had right about now. I'm generally not one to be self-conscious or lack confidence, but the way this man carries himself with such control and self-assurance has me wavering a little.

He isn't much taller than me, but for some reason, I feel much smaller at this moment. I inhale quickly, breathing in the hint of sunscreen mixed with a spicy masculine scent.

Damn, he smells good.

"How long are you here for?" I inquire, keeping the conversation light and trying to put forth a boldness I'm not sure I have. This man is more intimidating than I thought he would be but in a good way.

"Two more days," he informs me. "You?"

"I got here yesterday and have six more days to go."

"How about we take advantage of the two days we have left together, then?" he suggests, placing his hand on my chest and running his fingers down my torso, teasing the waistband of my bottoms when he reaches it.

I suck in a deep inhale as my cock starts to swell—which everyone can see in detail since my Speedo does nothing to hide it—before grinning at him and tilting my head to the side. Time to channel my fuck-boy ways and show him I'm here to have a good time. "Sounds like a solid plan to me. Your room or mine?"

He chuckles, shaking his head. "Let's finish our drinks first. We can pick a room once we're done."

Has anyone I've hooked up with in the past suggested we take things slow once I've offered sex? I don't think so, but more alcohol doesn't sound like a bad plan. "Want to sit somewhere shaded?" I ask, my skin already crisping from the punishing sun. "Or you could rub me up with some more sunscreen. Whatever floats your boat." I wink at him.

He licks his lips, causing prickles of anticipation to erupt across my skin. The things this man could probably do with that tongue have me squirming with desire.

"I do love the idea of my hands all over your body, and I'm going to make that happen soon, but why don't we hang out in the shade for now? That way, I don't get a mouthful of sunscreen when I trace each of your abs with my tongue later."

My cock likes that idea—a lot—stiffening even more from his words. Of course, the sexy stranger takes that moment to trail his eyes over my body again, taking in my growing erection. A low growl pours from his mouth before he bites his lower lip.

I'm practically vibrating with need when he tilts his chin. "Come on, there's a free table over there."

I eagerly follow him and almost melt when he puts his hand on my lower back, guiding me away from the bar. His touch isn't cautious, and his confidence has me sucking in a breath. I've always loved a man who likes to take control, even if I don't give it up easily in the bedroom. I can't wait to see what the universe has planned for us. Hopefully, it involves hot-as-sin sex.

"My name's Ian, by the way. What's yours?" he asks, pulling a chair out for me at a shaded table.

Damn. Also a gentleman? Could he be any sexier?

Taking our seats, Ian sits in the chair across the table from me, and I consider what name to give him. Typically, I'd use the nickname all my teammates and pretty much everyone I know calls me back home. For some reason, it doesn't seem right. "Ben," I respond after some contemplation, giving my real name which is a little weird on my tongue from lack of use.

"Ben," he purrs, his voice sending delicious shocks directly to my cock. Have I ever been this turned-on by someone so quickly? Maybe it has just been too long since I've gotten laid, and anything and anyone would be getting me this hot and bothered. Or maybe it's just this man.

"It's a simple name, but it suits you," he tells me, and I find my cheeks heating from the compliment.

Ian's voice is deep and smooth like butter.

Does it change when he's in bed with somebody?

I'm dying to find out. Is he a dirty talker?

I fucking hope so.

"What made you come out here all by yourself?" I question, sipping on my beer.

"Likely the same thing as you," he responds. "I needed a break from reality for a couple of days and wanted to do that in a place where I'm free to be unapologetically who I am. Of course, I was also hoping I'd meet a sexy guy like yourself who'd let me fuck him until he can't walk straight."

A shiver of desire rushes down my spine. Fuck, he has a way with words and the ability to turn someone on with his mouth alone. I love a man like that. I'm bi, but when I am with a man, I want someone to fuck me senseless and be the dirtiest talker around. I'm pretty sure Ian is exactly my type.

"Tell me more about yourself," I press and sip more of my beer even though the desire to chug it and say *fuck talking* is strong.

"Do you really want to get to know me better, or are you just being polite?" he questions with a lifted brow, and his lips quirk upward.

His sky-blue eyes stare at me intently, which makes me wiggle in my chair a little, and I shrug. "You were the one who suggested we sit and finish our drinks," I remind him, making him laugh lightly.

"I guess you're not wrong," he replies. "I'll be honest, I'm kind of a boring person in my day-to-day life."

"Does that mean you'll bore me in bed too?" I tease.

His tongue runs across his upper teeth, and his pupils dilate, causing his eyes to appear a little darker at my sassy response. "I promise I'm anything but boring in bed."

Deciding I've had enough conversation, I chug the rest of my beer, leaning onto the table. "How 'bout you show me what you got then," I encourage. "Unless you're all talk and no action."

The smile that spreads across his face is almost devilish, and I wonder if I made a mistake by poking the bear. "I promise you, baby. I know what I'm doing." His voice is smooth like silk, leaving me all hot and bothered, but I refuse to let that show just yet.

"Prove it," I challenge, raising one of my eyebrows.

With a smooth motion, he pushes the chair back, standing and offering his hand to me. "You've got a bratty side, don't you?" he checks as I take his hand.

"Maybe, is that going to be a problem?"

He chuckles and shakes his head, pulling me into his arms. "Not at all. It's only going to be that much more fun to tame you."

"Many have tried, but none have succeeded," I sass with a smirk.

"I love a challenge," he murmurs, smashing his lips to mine.

He immediately takes control, sliding his tongue into my mouth and twirling it around mine. My cock throbs in the confines of my bathing suit. I'm desperate to be naked with this man *now*. I shift my hips forward, pressing my erection into his thigh, which causes Ian to growl.

"My room, *now*," he commands, grabbing my hand and pulling me along.

I snicker but don't complain. I'm beyond fucking excited to have this man show me what he's got. I'm keeping my fingers crossed he isn't all talk and no action because that would be a huge disappointment. Thankfully, I have six days to find someone new if he turns out to be a dud.

When we arrive at his room, he lets us in, then immediately shoves me against the wall, his mouth once again on mine. The kiss is even more demanding and grueling this time. His teeth nip at my lip, causing me to moan into his mouth when he pushes his hard cock against mine.

"You're so fucking hot," he tells me, trailing kisses along my jaw, down to my neck, then lower, stopping at my nipples to give them some attention.

"Fuuuccckkk," I hiss out when he bites my left nipple, my head falling back with a thud against the wall.

He stays at my chest for who knows how long, licking, sucking, and biting. Ian is taking his time with my body, even though I'm desperate for him to fuck me or even just suck me already. But something tells me if I try to force him to hurry, he'll only slow his pace even more, which is the exact opposite of what I want to happen, so I call on all the patience I have, letting him have his way with me.

I've been told orgasms are stronger the longer you have to wait, but I've never tested the theory. I guess I'm going to find out today if it's true.

I'm not sure how long has passed when Ian finally drops to his knees, tracing my abs with his tongue, as he promised earlier. His mouth is close to where I want it but too fucking far away at the same time. My patience is dwindling at a rapid speed, and I thrust my hips forward, desperate for him to grab my cock already.

Ian clicks his tongue. "Do you need me to slow down some more?" he questions.

I shake my head quickly, rubbing the back of it against the wall as I do. "I need you to touch me already," I plead.

When I cast my eyes down at him, he has that devilish smile on his face once again. "I am touching you, baby," he replies, running his hands up and down my outer thighs. He then glides his tongue along the waistband of my Speedo. "What more do you need?"

"I need to be naked with your mouth on my cock," I demand.

He runs his nose along my throbbing cock, over the thin swim fabric. "But I'm having too much fun how we are right now," he explains. "Are you sure you want this to be over with already? I promise if you keep letting me set the pace, this will be the best sexual experience of your life."

I want to argue, but I'm also curious to see what he means. I'm not normally submissive in the bedroom. I am more of a bossy bottom who likes to be in control while still getting my insides rearranged, but for some reason, the idea of giving up that power to Ian is intriguing.

"Okay," I whisper, taking a deep, shaky inhale.

"Good boy," he praises. The words make my cock jolt,

pushing the material of my swimsuit forward which has Ian grinning. "Somebody likes to be praised."

I was unaware I had a thing for praise until this moment. No one has called me a good boy before, but his words triggered something inside me. Now, I'm desperate to be the *best* boy for him. However, I'm sure I'll return to my bratty ways soon enough.

"I'm going to free your cock now, but I want you to stay statue still," he instructs, his fingers digging into my waistband. "Can you do that for me?" I nod, but Ian clicks his tongue again. "Words, baby."

"I can be still," I assure him. "I'll be a good boy."

This might be my first time giving up control in a situation like this, but I'm determined to give it my all. I want to explore this new side of myself I'm just now discovering, and Ian seems like the perfect man to do that with.

He hums his praise. "Yes, you will be because you're eager to please me, aren't you?"

"Yes…" I pause, then try a word that's on the tip of my tongue since he called me a good boy and very clearly is a dominant kind of man. "… Daddy." Once the word falls past my lips, I hold my breath, praying I made the right call and not jumping the gun using a title like that. Honestly, I'm not even sure why that word popped into my head. It just did, and it felt right. Now, I have to pray Ian likes it as much.

He growls low in his throat, sending chills of desire to course through my veins. *Fuck, how do I get him to make that sound again?*

"That word sounds fucking perfect from your mouth," he tells me, easing all my worries. "I can't wait to hear you scream it when I'm balls deep inside you."

In a fluid motion, Ian rids me of my Speedo, finally allowing my cock some freedom. As the material slips down my legs, I kick out of it and my sandals at the same time.

"So sexy," he murmurs, trailing his tongue from my balls

to my tip, swirling it around the crown when he gets to the head.

It takes all my strength to stay still, but I don't want to disobey Ian.

"Keep your eyes on me," he instructs, staring intently into mine.

"Yes, D-d-daddy," I whisper, trying the word for a second time and noticing how it causes a spark of lust-filled desire to light his eyes.

I've never called a man Daddy before today, but I'll admit I'm more than enjoying this exchange with Ian.

"Daddy's going to suck your needy cock, but you are not allowed to come, do you understand?"

"Yes, Daddy," I repeat.

The title still feels foreign on my tongue, but not unwanted. It's turning me on more than I ever would have thought possible. Who knew I'd enjoy being submissive and had a praise and Daddy kink? I wasn't expecting to learn so much about myself during this trip, but I'm not complaining.

"Good boy," he murmurs, taking my throbbing erection into his warm, wet mouth.

"Shit," I gasp out, gripping his head with both my hands.

Ian swallows me deep down, my length sliding into his throat, causing electric shocks to shoot through my body. *Holy. Shit.* He doesn't have a gag reflex. I've never been with someone who can take all of me in one go.

I've always prided myself on my stamina, but Ian's talented mouth pushes me to my limits. I curl my toes into the carpet and try my hardest to resist the orgasm that is building deep in my balls.

"Daddy," I plead, this time the title falling almost instinctively. "I want to be a good boy, but if you keep that up, I'm going to blow."

Ian pauses, slowly sliding up my cock, allowing it to fall out of his mouth.

"Thank you for telling me," he praises. "You're not used to edging, are you?"

I shake my head. "This is a first. Most guys I've been with want to get down and dirty as soon as possible."

"How old are you?" he asks, nuzzling my thigh.

"Twenty."

He hums. "That makes more sense then. You're used to quick fucks. I was like that at your age too. How 'bout I let you come in my mouth, then we can move this to the bed, where I'll play with you some more. You'll be allowed to have your second orgasm when I'm balls deep inside you."

"Yes, please," I breathe out, trying not to sound too eager.

He chuckles, lapping at my cock again. "But remember to stay still, baby. I'm the one in charge. If you buck those hips, I'll stop, and you won't reach that high you're desperate for."

"I'll be still. I promise."

He smiles and nods, his brows raised expectantly. "You will because you're a good boy, and you like it when Daddy takes control, don't you?"

Typically, my repones would be a resounding *hell no*. I've always been the one in charge, and I thought that was how I was always going to like it, but clearly, things have changed, or at least they're different right now anyway.

I bite my lip and bob my head, whispering, "Yes, Daddy."

How is it that calling this man Daddy is so easy for me? You'd think I'd be struggling with this dynamic. Not only am I using an honorific I've never used, but I'm also submitting for the first time. It's almost like second nature. I must have had this side to me all along and just needed a talented older man like Ian to unlock it.

"Come when you're ready," he instructs, sucking my hard length into his mouth once again.

My head falls back, but he doesn't reprimand me for not holding eye contact this time. At least I'm able to keep the rest of my body still, for the time being, anyway.

Ian is a fucking master with his mouth, swallowing my cock down his throat and using the constriction to choke it in a toe-curling way.

"Fuck yes," I cry out when he picks up speed.

His slurps and hums fill the otherwise silent space. I love it. My moans and whimpers become louder, echoing in the room, the closer I am to my release.

"I-I'm close," I stammer, my balls drawing up, and a tingle shoots up my spine.

Ian's eyes meet mine again like he's silently giving me the go-ahead to let go, and I do, shouting so fucking loud my throat burns a little.

My head spins as I shoot my load down Ian's throat, and he swallows every last drop. I've never experienced an orgasm that intense in my entire life. If that was just from a blow job, what is it going to be like when he fucks me?

"Ready to take this to the bed?" Ian asks, rising to his feet, still licking his lips.

It takes me a second to process what he's asked since I'm trying to catch my breath and coming down from such an incredible high. "Do you mind if I have a shower first?" I request when I'm able to form a sentence again. I want to be extra clean for him when he takes my ass.

His lips turn up in that confident grin of his, and he dips his chin. "You can, but don't take too long."

The instant I have his permission, I rush to the bathroom with a giant grin on my face. This might only be a summer fuck, but I'm glad I met Ian today. He allowed me to discover new things about myself that I probably wouldn't have figured out otherwise.

CHAPTER TWO

Ian

IT HAS BEEN a long time since I've been with someone in their early twenties, but Ben doesn't disappoint, not even in the slightest. He's hot as sin and eager to please. And I'm more than willing to teach him some new things.

"How old are you?" Ben asks, walking out of the bathroom with a towel wrapped around his waist.

"Thirty-one. Do you mind the age gap?"

He shakes his head. "Not at all. People say that older men know what they're doing. Now I'm able to confirm that's the truth."

I chuckle. "I'm glad I'm satisfying you so far."

He licks his lips, dipping his chin. "I'm more than satisfied, but I'm also ready for you to show me if your dick is as talented as your mouth."

I chuckle again, then tilt my head, gesturing for him to join me. I'm beyond pleased when he drops his towel and steps forward. The second he's within arm's reach, I pull him in for a searing kiss, enjoying the way he quickly melts into my embrace.

I wasn't sure how submissive Ben would be when we first met at the bar, considering how upfront and honest he was about wanting to fuck. Obviously, some submissives are forward, but I also wouldn't have put it past Ben to be a power bottom.

To say the least, I've been pleasantly surprised with how well he lets me take the lead. And when he called me Daddy for the first time, I almost came in my pants. The way he tentatively said it, I'm sure it was a first for him, but I'm always up for showing boys new sides to themselves.

"Lay on your stomach," I instruct, pulling away so he's able to obey, which he does quickly. I'm not sure how much experience Ben has with being submissive, but he's proving to be excellent at it.

With smooth movements, I position myself behind him, straddling his legs. His muscles are tight beneath my hands while I kneed his bubble butt, pulling his cheeks apart to reveal his sexy pucker.

This boy is so hot it should be illegal. His body is strong and toned. *What does he do to keep it in pristine shape like this?* You don't get a body like this from sitting on the couch all day. Take it from me, I work my butt off to keep in shape, but even I don't have muscles like this boy does.

Desperate to taste his cake, I lower myself, giving him a long, slow lick, smiling when he shivers. I hum to show my appreciation of how delicious he tastes before lapping at him again, and again, and again.

Ben's moans fill the room, becoming louder as I lick his hole and nibble at his rim. I've always had a thing for loud lovers, and Ben is proving to be exactly what I crave in a man.

I stiffen my tongue, shoving it inside Ben's entrance, swirling it around to soften him. One of my favorite things about sex is the buildup and the foreplay.

Obviously, I've had my fair share of quick fucks, but that isn't what I enjoy anymore. I want to take my time with the boys I bring to my bed. I want to tease them and turn them into whimpering messes before I fuck them so hard they struggle to walk straight.

Unfortunately, I haven't had the time to do that in what feels like forever. I've been working myself to the bone, trying to prove to my colleagues and bosses that I'm good at what I do. It's been paying off, but my personal life has become obsolete because of it.

This is why I was desperate to run away this summer. And boy, am I glad I did. I've been at this resort for five days now and was beginning to give up hope of finding a guy who checked off all my boxes. I've met plenty of sexy men here, but none that instantly turned me on like Ben did. I almost brought back a few to my room, but something always stopped me.

With Ben it was different. The connection was instant. Nothing in the back of my head was shouting to put the brakes on.

I take my time fucking Ben's ass with my tongue, relishing in his unique taste. Have I ever tasted anything this delicious? If I have, it's been far too long.

Once I feel like he's ready, I suck on my fingers, getting them good and wet so I'm able to stretch his hole. I don't have the world's largest cock, but if I don't at least give this sexy boy a quick prep, it's going to hurt, which isn't what I want. I like to fuck hard, but I'm not about causing intense pain.

"Yesss," Ben hisses out when I slide in my first finger.

"Damn, you're tight. How long has it been since you've had anything in this perfect channel?" I inquire.

"It's been a hot minute," he shares. "Life has been busy."

His words hit deep in my bones. Clearly, I'm not the only one who has put their personal life on the back burner. But how busy could a twenty-year-old's life really be? He's probably in college, but doesn't that normally entail studying a little and partying as hard as you can? Even if he took his studies seriously and wasn't into the party scene, I still can't see how he wouldn't have the time to mess around. Part of me wants to find out what he has going on in his life that is stopping him from living as freely as he should at his age, but this is just a hookup, not a relationship.

I push away the desire to get to know him on a level I probably shouldn't and get my head back in the game.

I need to spend extra time getting this sexy boy ready, which is no hardship at all. I massage one ass cheek with my free hand and slide in a second finger. It might have been a while for him, but it's obvious he is not a virgin with how quickly he relaxes his muscles.

Scissoring my fingers, I lick at his rim again, allowing my tongue to slide inside once more, ensuring he stays nice and wet.

"So fucking good." He pants as I continue to fuck him with my tongue and fingers. His hips tremble every once in a while, telling me he is trying his hardest not to hump the bed, which fills my chest with pride. I love that he knows I wouldn't want him doing that.

"Are you ready for my cock?" I ask, fucking him with my fingers and nailing his prostate a couple of times.

"God, yes!" he cries out. "Fuck me, Daddy, please!"

I love how the title falls from his lips with ease this time.

"Mmm... that's my good needy boy! Now move to the edge of the bed and position yourself on your hands and knees," I instruct, sliding my fingers out and getting off the bed to collect a condom and bottle of lube.

When I turn around, Ben is already in position, making me grin.

With ease, I tear open the condom wrapper and sheath my erection. "You're so fucking sexy," I state, strutting toward him, rubbing my hand up his spine once I'm close enough to touch him. "You've been such a good boy for me. Are you ready for your reward?"

He hums in response, lapping up my words of praise. "Yes, Daddy."

I pour a dollop of lube onto my fingers and rub his beautiful pucker before slipping them into his greedy hole, making sure he's nice and slick.

"Please, Daddy," he begs when I don't instantly slide my dick in.

"Patience, baby. I don't want to hurt you," I state. "You want this to feel good, don't you?"

He nods. "Yes, but I just want to be filled with your cock. Please, fuck me, Daddy."

I pull my fingers out and stroke my dick with the excess lube.

"I love it when you use your manners," I croon, lining my cock up with his entrance. "I'm not going to be gentle. If you're not ready, tell me now."

"I'm ready, fuck me so hard I'll be feeling it for the rest of my stay here," he pleads.

I can't stop the growl that crawls up my chest at his words. I love a boy who isn't afraid to voice what he wants.

With a firm grip on his hips, I thrust forward, sliding into his warm channel with a groan.

"Sooo goood," Ben cries out when I bury myself deep inside him.

"It's only going to get better," I assure him before pounding into him like I promised.

My balls smack against his taint as I fuck him hard and fast. I've spent my time teasing and pleasuring my boy, and now it's time to let loose. I don't care how fast either of us come because, either way, it's going to be mind-blowingly good.

With grueling thrusts, I pound into Ben with everything I have. His cries of pleasure let me know he's enjoying this as much as I am.

Sweat covers our bodies, and I'm panting hard as I keep my pace. When my balls start to draw up, I reach under Ben's body to stroke his cock. My fist slides up and down his dick in movements that match my hips, and his whimpers become even louder.

"Are you close?" I check.

"Y-y-yes," he stammers, sounding desperate to let go.

"Give it to me, baby."

It's like my words have the power to send him over the edge because he shouts, shooting his load and covering the bed with his thick seed.

His channel clamps down around my cock with his orgasm, drawing my release.

"Fuck," I yell, coming so hard my head spins a little. It's been a long time since I've had an orgasm this intense.

I continue to buck my hips until my cock is spent. Only then do I still and slowly slide out of the sexy boy who has collapsed into the pile of his cum. Clearly, I fucked him good enough for his limbs to give out.

"Want another shower, then grab a bite to eat?" I check with Ben, who flashes me a satiated grin.

"Sounds like a solid plan. Maybe you should call room service to clean your bedding," he suggests.

I laugh. "That's not a bad idea."

I help Ben up, pulling him into my arms and kissing him gently before we head to the bathroom.

Ben is exactly the type of boy I would want in my life full-time. But any man deserves better than what I have to offer. That's why I don't have a boyfriend. I'll just have to soak up the couple of days I have with Ben.

CHAPTER THREE

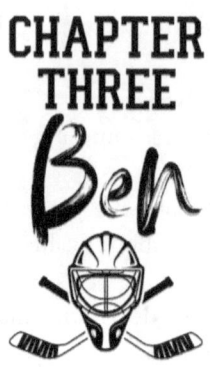

ALMOST THREE MONTHS LATER

THE SCHOOL YEAR has officially started, and things are already crazy intense.

Hockey season starts in about a month, but pre-season practice is already well underway. I'm also working with a coaching team to better my abilities as a goalie.

I've worked on getting stronger all summer, except for the one week I took off to relax in paradise. I'll never forget Ian or the two days we spent together. But now, my focus is solely on hockey and my grades, which is why I told Ian I didn't want to exchange information. But if I'm being honest with myself, I've regretted that decision ever since. I have the ability to focus on my grades, play killer hockey, *and* get railed by the hottest Daddy ever.

Hockey has always been a sport that comes easy, and I bet I'd still be a good player even if I slacked off, but that isn't the type of person I am. When I join something, I put my all into it. I don't half-ass anything. So, even though I have no desire to play hockey professionally, I'm determined to give it my all while I play at the college level.

The Green Spring Koalas hockey team has won the championship for the last two years, and I'm determined to secure a third win before I'm no longer eligible to play. Even if it were possible to play next year, my focus would still need to be on schooling since I enter med school then.

Ever since I was a kid, I knew I wanted to be a doctor. When I discovered a way to mix that with my love for all sports, I was sold on going into sports medicine. It's a long fucking process, but I know I'm capable.

Some people call me crazy for not wanting to pursue hockey professionally, but it was never my dream. I enjoy playing, and while I'm in college, I'll play my heart out, but when it's over, I won't be sad to give it up.

"Have you seen the hot new professor?" one of my new roommates, Nick Bronson, or Bronny for short, asks when he gets home.

Bronny is gay, so he's obviously not talking about a female teacher. He's a freshman and a wrestler but an overall cool guy.

I shake my head. "What course is he teaching?" I inquire.

"First-year writing," Bronny responds.

"Yeah, I took that my first year, so I doubt I'll meet him." I stare at him for a moment and cock my head to the side. "Wait, how hot are we talking?"

My roommate blushes and shrugs. "Hotter than any teacher I've ever seen."

"Damn. Think you can sneak me a pic?" I ask with a smirk.

He shakes his head. "I don't want to get in shit."

I pat him on the shoulder in understanding. It's tough being a freshman.

"It's all good. Maybe I'll pick you up from class next week and sneak in the back once the class gets let out. If a teacher is *that* hot, I've got to see him for myself. What time does your class end?"

Bronny chuckles. "Sounds like a solid plan. It's my class just before lunch. It ends around eleven forty-five," he tells me.

"Excellent. I don't have any morning classes this semester, so I'll be able to swing that no problem."

"Cool, did you want to hit the gym in a little bit?" he asks.

"Sure. I had to skip my workout this morning. I could use at least an hour in the gym," I explain.

"Yeah. I'm not looking forward to getting up at the ass crack of dawn to work out once the wrestling season starts," Bronny grumbles. "But if I don't do the work and take it to the next level, I'm not going to impress anyone. I kind of made a name for myself in high school wrestling and want to keep that up at the college level."

"I understand, man. Being a freshman sucks, but you'll get the hang of it eventually," I encourage him.

"Can someone please explain why everyone is talking about first-year writing like it's the best thing since sliced bread?" Rio, my other new roommate, asks, walking through the door.

"Rumor on the street is there is a hot new professor," I tell Rio, and Bronny dips his chin.

"He's like the child of a Greek god or something," Bronny explains, letting out a dreamy sigh, making Rio and I laugh.

"Anyone got a picture?" Rio asks.

"He probably has a picture on the faculty website," Bronny offers, but I shake my head and slice my hand through the air.

"Those pictures are shit. It won't be good enough. We've got to see this guy in real life. I'm gonna sneak in next week when I pick Bronny up for lunch. Want to join?" I ask Rio, who shrugs.

"I don't think I have anything going on, so sure, I'll join in," he states.

Rio is demisexual, which means he's not going to get a hard-on like the rest of us, but he's still able to appreciate someone's beauty.

"Excellent, it sounds like a plan. Now Bronny and I should probably head to the gym before we lose our gumption."

"Have fun. I'm going to study," Rio says, heading to the living room with his backpack.

"Come on, Bronny, let's go pump some iron," I joke with a pat on his shoulder.

I'm extremely intrigued to find out what this hot professor looks like. It's too bad I have to wait an entire week to find out.

CHAPTER FOUR

Ian

MY CLASS IS FULL, which isn't normal for first-year writing, considering most kids dread this required class, putting it off as long as they can.

I'll take it as a win. I'm eager to show my new bosses they made the right call by hiring me.

I've been a professor for three years, and when GSU offered me a position, I was blown away. I'm now on the tenure track and am determined to show everyone they didn't make a mistake.

"Professor Johnson," a female with long, blonde hair says, raising her hand. I believe her name is Mindy, but I'm still learning everyone's names.

"Yes?"

"Are you single?" she asks, batting her lashes at me and making the entire class laugh. On the other hand, I can't help but sigh.

"My personal life doesn't matter because even if I was, I don't date students," I state with a firm tone, turning my focus to the entire class. "I'm your professor and ally when it comes to your studies, but I am not your friend. I would very much appreciate it if all of you would refrain from asking any more personal questions."

The class mutters an acceptance of my statement, and I continue teaching the lesson at hand. With a press of the button on the remote in my hand, the screen at the front of the class changes slides, and all eyes are now where they need to be.

Not on me.

While I speak, I try to remain engaging and confident, hoping that if the students love the subject enough, they'll forget about me. Thankfully, it seems to work because no one pries into my personal life for the rest of the period.

"Have a great rest of your day," I call out to everyone when class ends.

I lean against my desk, arms folded across my chest, watching the students shuffle out of the class. But what catches my attention the most is two young men who are entering while the majority are leaving. The gasp that leaves my lips can't be stifled when one of the young men turns around, and our eyes meet. His blond brows shoot up, and he appears just as conflicted as I am.

What is Ben doing here? Please, God, tell me he isn't one of my students.

He's talking with the man he entered with and another one I recognize from class today, but I don't remember his name. While the guys talk, Ben pulls out a notebook, writes something down, and then walks in my direction.

"What are you doing, Coop?" my student hisses at Ben, but he waves him off.

"Hi, Professor Johnson, it's nice to meet you," Ben says with one hand in his pocket, his shoulder hunched a little like he's nervous, which I understand why he would be. I highly doubt he was expecting to run into me today. He holds his other hand out tentatively, and I stare at it like it's going to bite me. "I'm Ben Cooper, but everyone around here calls me Coop. If you like hockey, our team is the best, and you should definitely come to one of our games."

Carefully, I take his hand, giving it a firm handshake, ignoring the electric jolts that shoot up my arm. Between his palm and mine is a small piece of paper he tore off before coming to speak to me, and I'm careful not to drop it when I let go of his hand.

"It's nice to meet you, Mr. Cooper. I've never been a big hockey fan, but I do like to support our students. Maybe I'll attend a game one day. Are you one of my students?" I check, making sure to keep my tone even, not wanting to clue anyone into the fact that we know each other intimately.

Ben shakes his head. "Nope, I took this class my first year. I only stopped by to pick up my friend for lunch. I thought it would be rude not to introduce myself. I guess I'll see you around," he says, heading back to his friends, whispering harshly at him.

Once they leave and my classroom is empty, I open the piece of paper.

It's his phone number and below it, he wrote, *Call me.*

I've never been involved with a student, and even though he isn't *my* student, he's still a student at this university. Do I want to cross that line? I'm not sure. Yet I don't throw the note away, either. Instead, I slip it into my pocket, collect my things, and head out for lunch. I'll figure out what to do with the number later.

CHAPTER FIVE

IS this real life right now, or am I dreaming?

"Why did you introduce yourself to my professor?" Bronny whisper-shouts as we walk to my car, giving me a shove along the way.

Okay, I felt that, so this must be real life, which is fucking crazy. Never in a million years did I think I would find Ian when I entered Bronny's class today.

I'm also not sure what gave me the strength to give him my number, but it felt like I had to at the same time. I've been dreaming about Ian since we parted ways, and it seemed like fate was giving me a second chance, and I had to take it. It was a risky move, but I'm praying it was worth it.

"I was just inviting him to watch a hockey game once the season starts. Is it really such a big deal?"

"Professor Johnson made a big deal about not dating students, and then you went up and flirted with him," Bronny grumbles.

"Well, I'm not *his* student, am I?" I counter. "Besides, I wasn't flirting." Okay, that was a lie, but what Bronny doesn't know won't hurt him.

"Coop flirting with your professor isn't going to harm your grade if you're worried about that," Rio assures Bronny.

Oh shit, I hadn't figured Bronny would be worried about me harming his grade.

"Is that what you were thinking?" I ask him, and he shrugs.

"My grades are important to me," he murmurs.

"I promise that even if I *was* flirting with your professor, it won't reflect poorly on you," I assure him. "Besides, he didn't come across upset when I invited him to a hockey game."

My words appear to settle his nerves, and he nods. "Okay, what are you buying me for lunch?" he requests, and I laugh.

"How 'bout a sandwich at the café on the other side of campus?" I offer, making his face light up like a child on Christmas morning.

"They have my *favorite* sandwich there," he says, and I swear a little drool forms at the corner of his mouth.

"Then let's go. I've got classes this afternoon, and I don't have time to doddle around," I tease.

As I drive us to the café, I can't stop thinking about Ian. *Will he call me? What happens if he does? What kind of relationship will we be able to have with both of us living busy lives? Would I even want a relationship or just someone to fuck me so hard I forget my name?*

My mind is racing a mile a minute, and by the time we arrive at the café, I'm no closer to an answer to my questions than when I started.

MY PHONE IS SITTING on the coffee table, and I keep staring at it like I've suddenly developed superpowers and can make Ian call with the strength of my mind. Of course, that doesn't happen.

"Why do you keep staring at your phone?" Rio asks from the rocking chair where he's watching television.

I'm also supposed to be paying attention to the show, but my thoughts keep drifting to Ian. I'm an idiot to hope he'll actually call. Even if I'm not *his* student, I bet there is a policy preventing all student-faculty relationships, which is stupid because we're all adults here. He has no power to make me pass or fail a class. Why is it wrong for us to have a relationship?

"I was hoping someone would call," I reply with a shrug. "But I'm not sure if that's going to happen."

Rio fakes a gasp. "Is Playboy Coop being rejected for the first time ever?"

I roll my eyes, flipping him the bird.

I've had a reputation as a playboy for the past three years, but maybe I've outgrown those days. Sure, I love sex, and I don't have time for a relationship, so it's worked well, but sleeping with a different guy or girl every night doesn't have the same appeal it once did. Maybe it's time I find someone open to a friends-with-benefits type relationship.

Of course, the first person who pops into my head as I think about that is Ian. Not that we're even friends, but I'd like to change that if he gives me the chance.

I just don't see that happening.

CHAPTER SIX

IT'S BEEN a week since Ben walked into my classroom and handed me his phone number—seven days where I haven't been able to get him out my mind. So many times, I should have thrown out said number but haven't been able to bring myself to do it. Instead, I programmed it into my phone and have been staring at the number for too long every night.

Here I am again, grading papers and casting glances at my phone.

Should I just send him a text already?

No.

I can't.

It goes against all my ethics.

I don't date students...

... *ever.*

Whether they are mine or not. The school would be fine with it as long as I filled out the proper paperwork. At least, that's what I assume. Yet, it still doesn't seem right.

Tell that to my fingers that are itching to reach for my phone and do it anyway.

Giving my head a shake, I ignore the desire to text him and continue to grade papers. Maybe with time, the urge to reach out will fade. I just have to push through and be strong.

I can do that.

Right?

THE HALLWAYS ARE ALWAYS PACKED with students, and I smile and wave at the familiar faces, not missing the way some students blush or whisper to their friends as they pass. I've been dubbed the *hot new teacher,* which is damn annoying, but there isn't anything I'm able to do about it except keep my boundaries clear.

"Funny seeing you here, Professor Johnson."

I instantly recognize the voice, and my body heats with desire, but I force my feet to keep moving.

"I struggle to see how it's funny, considering this is my place of employment," I state, and Ben steps in beside me, keeping pace.

"Well, I wouldn't have to hunt you down if you had just called," he tells me with a bratty smirk.

"I won't be calling you," I state quietly. Surprisingly, my voice is firm, not giving away what I really want.

"Why not?" he inquires, nibbling on his lower lip and looking a bit self-conscious, which makes me feel like a jerk. I don't want to upset him, but I can't give in either. "You wanted my number when you left the resort."

"That was before I knew you were going to be a student at this college," I reply, keeping my voice low.

"Did I cross a line?" he asks with furrowed brows and a slight frown.

Technically, he didn't because I hadn't set it yet, but I need to put the boundary in place now. Unfortunately, the university halls aren't the best place.

"We can't have this conversation here," I tell him and don't miss how his eyes light up a little.

"Where *do* you want to talk then?" he inquires with a small hopeful smile.

I press my fingers against my forehead. Frankly, I don't

want to have this conversation at all, but Ben deserves to know where I stand. I'm also pretty certain Ben won't drop this until I let him down gently but firmly.

"I'll text you with a time and place to meet. Now, if you'll excuse me, I have a class to prepare for."

I rush away, but not before noticing Ben's face light up at the suggestion of our meeting.

I am screwed when it comes to this boy.

My steps don't slow until I'm at my desk, where I text Ben, whom I've aptly named *Sweet Boy* in my contacts.

> Me: Meet me at this address tonight at eight o'clock.

I send my address in a separate message, making it easier for him to pull up in GPS. No sooner does the message read delivered than his reply comes through.

> Sweet Boy: I'll be there. What should I wear?

I blow out a breath at Ben's brazenness. He was mostly coy and sweet in the hall, but he's still very obviously a brat through and through. If he were actually my boy, I'd love the attitude and the way he pushes my buttons. But he's not, so it's only frustrating because there is nothing I'm able to do to correct his behavior. I can't spank him or edge him until he apologizes. No, I have to be professional.

It's killing me.

> Me: Wear what you were wearing when I ran into you in the hall. This conversation won't take long. I just don't want people eavesdropping.

> Sweet boy: We'll see about that. Talk soon, Daddy.

My cock grows at the word, hearing his voice in my head. I'll never forget how he panted that honorific when he was begging to come.

Inviting Ben to my house tonight will most likely turn out to be a mistake, but I'm out of options. I need to explain I'm not willing to cross this line, but the school isn't the best place to have this conversation since there are people who could overhear us and report it to the dean.

Thankfully, it doesn't take long for my students to begin making their way into my classroom, effectively distracting me from thoughts of Ben.

I'll deal with him later.

Right now, I have a job to do that doesn't include fantasizing about him.

CHAPTER SEVEN

PRACTICE TODAY WAS fun and exhilarating, but multiple times throughout, my thoughts drifted to Ian and tonight. Thankfully, I didn't let that affect my play.

When the puck was flying my way, my head was in the game, but every time we broke for water or for the coaches to correct a play, I found myself thinking about what could possibly happen tonight.

A NERVOUS AND excited energy runs through my veins as I head to the address Ian texted. I'm sure he's planning on telling me we can't be together, but that won't happen if I have any say in the matter.

I like Ian a lot, and I'm certain he likes me too. At least, he did when we were parting ways at the resort. While we did spend a lot of time fucking, we also got to know each other. We shared meals and talked about nothing and everything. We didn't really discuss our careers like we were both trying to forget about that stuff for a while, but we did have conversations about other things, like our favorite animals and what we would do with our lives if money wasn't a problem.

I learned so much about myself over those two days, and

it was all thanks to Ian. There has to be a way to make this work. I just have to convince him it's a good idea.

When I pull up to the address, I'm surprised to find a decent-sized house. Honestly, I was expecting something on the smaller side, not a place big enough to raise a family. I fucking hope Ian doesn't have a secret family. That would definitely have me changing plans. I don't mess around with married men or anyone in a relationship, for that matter. I might be a manwhore, but I don't participate in cheating.

I take a deep breath, slowly blowing it out before walking to Ian's front door.

"Eight o'clock on the dot," Ian notes when he opens the door.

"Do you like my punctuality?" I ask.

"It's appreciated," he says, stepping to the side. "Why don't we have a seat in the living room? Like I told you in the text, this won't take long."

I follow him, staring at his lean back and pin-straight posture, like it always is.

He carries himself as a confident and dominant man, which in turn triggers me into a more submissive role that I don't experience with anyone else. Around anyone else, I act a lot like Ian does, with confidence and a swagger that has earned me the attention of many.

With my shoulders rounded, I sit next to him on the couch, so close our legs rub together. Obviously, I could have given him more space, but I didn't want to. I mean, at least I didn't perch myself on his lap, right? I might be submissive around him, but I'm still me, and I want to make my intentions known.

"I was hoping to talk in your bedroom," I tease, trying out the bratty side of myself that Ian told me he liked when we were at the resort.

Ian shakes his head, scootching away. "Ben, we can't do

this," he states, and his words hit me square in the chest like a dagger.

My gaze drops to the floor. I might want to fuck him so bad it hurts, but I do respect boundaries, most of the time. "Why not?" I counter, needing to hear an explanation.

When he was leaving the resort and asked for my number, it sounded like he wanted something, but I wasn't ready then. Honestly, I'm not sure I'm ready now, but I do know I want him. I just don't know how much I can give. "You're not *my* professor."

Ian sighs. "You're right, but it's still ethically not right."

"Is there a rule against it?" I inquire. "Would you lose your job?"

He shakes his head, and my heart flutters with the smallest amount of hope. "You and I would have to fill out paperwork, but technically it is allowed. Most professors, however, don't cross that line."

"If you're not going to get fired for it, how come you're pushing me away? You know how good we are together," I remind him.

"Besides the fact that it doesn't look right, I don't have time for a boyfriend. I spend most of my nights grading papers and working on new lesson plans. I won't be able to give you what you need. You were right for not giving me your number when I asked because a relationship between us could never work."

"I don't need a boyfriend," I reply. "Like I told you at the resort, my life is crazy, but that doesn't mean we don't have needs. I was thinking more like a friends-with-benefits situation."

He stares at me for a moment, his gaze so intense it almost steals my breath. What is going through his head right now? Is he considering agreeing to this? Please, God, let him say yes.

"I don't think I can do that," he whispers, breaking the eye contact.

I want to beg, but I also have pride and am aware when enough is enough. I knew tracking him down in the hall today was a long shot, but it was also my last shot. If Ian doesn't want to be with me, I have to accept that.

"You have my number if you change your mind," I tell him, standing and heading toward the door.

When my hand touches the doorknob, I pause, wishing Ian would stop me, but he doesn't.

I have to be okay with that.

Maybe it's best that we don't pursue something new. That way, the memories of our two days together in paradise won't be tainted, and I can cherish them forever.

IT'S BEEN a little over a week since Ian shot me down, and of course, he's all I think about, which is why I'm at a house party on a Friday night with a beer in hand, hoping to find someone to take home tonight. I mean, what better way to get over someone than to get under someone else?

"Ready for hockey season to start?" Michael Danvers, better known as Dano, a football player, asks as I scan the crowd.

"Yeah. We're already practicing our asses off, but I like the thrill of winning or losing."

"I like that too. I've been training all summer. I'm ready to show the coaches that I'm better than ever," he tells me with a big grin.

I clap him on the shoulder. "That's awesome. I'm stoked to see what you got. But if you'll excuse me, I'm on the prowl tonight."

He chuckles. "Get it."

I wander to where a group of puck bunnies is sitting, but I quickly make a beeline in the opposite direction before they see me. For some reason, the idea of taking one of them home tonight curdles my stomach.

Maybe I need more to drink. A little liquid courage never hurt anyone. So, I make my way to where a group of guys are playing beer pong.

"Mind if I join?" I ask.

"Fuck yeah!" one of the guys yells, letting me join his team.

Before I know it, the world is swirling around me, and I'm laughing at a dumb joke I don't really understand.

"Maybe you should slow down," one of the guys suggests a few games later, and I nod, but my head is heavy, almost like it's going to fall off if I'm not careful.

"Good ideeba," I slur, making him laugh as I walk away.

Now would be a good time to try the puck bunnies again. With my beer goggles on, they might be appealing. But I still don't want to fuck any of them. I want to be railed by a sexy daddy. Preferably the one who has been starring in all my dreams. So, I pull my phone out of my back pocket and send off a text.

> Me: Heyyy, Profffessor Daadddyy.

There might be a couple too many letters in those words, but I shrug because who cares?

While I wait for his response, or lack of one if he chooses to ignore me, I head to the living room, plopping down in a comfy recliner. People are laughing, talking, and dancing around, but everything is kind of a blur. Maybe I drank a little too much. But you only live once, right?

My phone vibrates in my hand, and a sudden bout of giddiness rushes through me when I see who sent a text.

Professor Daddy: Are you drunk?

I giggle and shake my head, loving that I programmed Ian's name that way into my contacts.

Me: Nooo.

Me: I'm just hoppy!

I stare at my screen with squinted eyes. There's something wrong with that text, so I try again.

Me: Hippy

Nope, still not right. One more time.

Me: Happy!

I smile at my accomplishment. See? I'm capable of texting when I'm drunk, and no one will be the wiser.

Professor Daddy: Jesus Christ. Where are you?

I look around the room. *Where am I again?* This isn't my place, but I'm not exactly sure whose house it is.

Me: goood questionnn...

Ian's response is almost instant, and it makes me giggle again.

Professor Daddy: You're going to cause me to have an aneurysm. Tell me where you are.

"Duuude, where am I?" I ask a guy standing nearby, and he laughs.

"Parker's house," he supplies, and that name rings a bell.

> Me: I'mm at Parrkker's houssse.

I'm busy texting when a puck bunny struts over and sits on the armrest of the chair I am sitting in.

"Hey, Coop," she purrs.

I smile at her, but it wavers when the putrid smell of her thick perfume hits me, and I fight back the urge to gag.

"Hi," I reply, trying not to show my disgust as my phone vibrates again.

> Professor Daddy: Who's Parker?

> Me: A foootball pllayerrr.

"I'm really looking forward to watching you play again," the puck bunny says, running her finger over my arm. Goose bumps break out across my skin, but not the good kind.

"Cool. Do you know Pawker's address? I getting ride," I tell her, and her smile grows.

"Could I share it with you?"

I shake my head. "Sorry. I too dwunk. I don't tink I can even get it up," I lie.

She pouts but gives me the address anyway. "Next time you're not so drunk, you should call me," she suggests. "Do you still have my number?"

I nod even though I'm positive I don't have it, then text Ian the address. I'm not sure if he'll actually show up, but it's worth a shot. If he doesn't, I'll just sleep in this chair. I'm sure no one will give a fuck if I do.

Apparently, I must have passed out at some point and am woken by a shaking. "Your ride's here," the dude who told me I was at Parker's house says, and I stare at him, super confused.

Did I order a ride? Maybe I did and just forgot. I am pretty fucking drunk.

"Tanksss, man," I slur, stumbling toward the front of the house.

I stare at the cars, searching for a ride share, when my eyes land on Ian who is scowling hard. Shit, he's clearly pissed off. *How come I find him really sexy like this?*

"You came!" I cheer, climbing into the passenger seat.

"I shouldn't have," he grumbles, pulling away the second my seat belt is fastened.

"Arrre yooou gonna get in twouble?" I ask.

He shakes his head. "I doubt it. Most people were too drunk to recognize me. Where do you live?"

I stare out at the streetlights, trying to recall my address, but it doesn't come to me.

"Dunno," I finally respond, making Ian sigh.

Leaning my head against the cool glass, my eyes become heavy. My head is fuzzy, and I can't tell if it's the car's vibration or the lingering effects of the alcohol. Vaguely, it registers I'm supposed to tell Ian something, but before I can figure out what that is, my eyelids fall, and I drift off.

CHAPTER EIGHT

Ian

HUNTING Ben down and picking him up from that house party was stupid. If someone saw me driving Ben and reported it to the dean, I have no excuse for why I was doing it.

When I received his first text, I knew I had to get him to ensure he was safe. And even though this has the possibility to all blow up in my face, I'm glad he's with me.

I wish I knew where he lived. But Ben is too drunk to remember, which means I'll have to bring him back to my house for the night and decide what I'm going to do in the morning. At the very least, I will have to fill out some paperwork saying that Ben and I have a history so things don't bite either of us in the ass.

If tonight proves anything, it's that I'm addicted to Ben Cooper. If I wasn't, I could have ignored his texts, but the instant his contact information lit up my phone, I opened the text without hesitation.

For the last couple of weeks, since he's reentered my life, Ben has been all I've thought about, and it felt like fate when he finally texted me. I could say this will be the last time I do something stupid, but it won't be. Ben is my kryptonite.

When I pull into my driveway, Ben is snoring, and I give his shoulder a gentle shove. "We're here," I whisper, and he slowly opens one eye.

"Where's here?" he questions in a drunken yet sleepy voice.

"My house since you apparently forgot where you live. I have a spare bedroom for you to sleep off your drunken stupor in."

"I'd prefer your bedroom," he murmurs, unbuckling his seatbelt.

"You're too drunk for that," I tell him, and he shrugs before nearly falling out of my car when he opens the door.

I rush to his side to help him, shaking my head.

"How much did you have to drink?" I inquire.

"I no-no," he mumbles.

I sigh because there's no use in trying to pluck more information out of him until morning. But I am concerned he might get in trouble for underage drinking. That has to be against the rules for student athletes. But again, that's something I'll have to talk to him about when he's sober and able to form coherent thoughts.

Carefully, I help Ben into my house, guiding him to the spare bedroom. I leave him there briefly to grab a bottle of water and some aspirin. Heaven knows he's going to need those for his hangover tomorrow.

When I return, Ben is stripping out of his clothes, and I squeeze my eyes shut. "Why didn't you wait to do that?" I grumble, fighting the urge to stare at his perfect body. It wouldn't be right to ogle him while he's inebriated like this and unable to give consent to anything.

"I no wike cwoz," he argues, somehow sounding more drunk and equally as tired.

I exhale with a sigh, moving to set the water and aspirin on the nightstand, keeping my gaze off Ben. "Drink all of the water and take two aspirin," I command in a tone I hope he won't argue with.

"Yes, Daddy," he mumbles, grabbing the bottle of water.

Shaking my head, I wish he wouldn't call me that right now.

Ben unscrews the cap and guzzles down a good portion of the bottle, making me happy.

"If you need anything, let me know," I tell him, heading for the door.

He hums his agreement, and by the rustling of the blankets, I know he's climbing into bed. I want nothing more than to climb in with him and hold him, but I refuse to take advantage of someone who's had too much to drink, so I force my feet to walk out the door to my bedroom.

Thankfully, it's a Friday night, and I don't have to work tomorrow because I highly doubt I'm going to sleep well tonight. especially with the boy who has been invading all my dreams sleeping across the hall.

THE SUN WAKES me up way too early.

Even though I've barely slept, I won't be able to go back to sleep, so I throw on a pair of sweats and a ratty old T-shirt, then head to the kitchen to start a pot of coffee.

Once it's going, I head to check on Ben, quietly opening the door and peering in to make sure he's okay. He's still fast asleep, but he's kicked off the blankets and is lying spread eagle on the bed, his cock resting heavy against his thigh. My own dick thickens at the sight, and I instantly feel like a creep. Quickly, I close my eyes and softly shut the door, not wanting to disturb him, and head back to the kitchen.

Needing to keep myself busy, I start whipping up some pancakes. I'll be able to keep them warm in the oven for when Ben eventually wakes up. Heaven only knows when that will be. That boy drank a hell of a lot last night, and sleep will help him recover.

While I cook, my thoughts keep drifting to my time with Ben at the resort. Never in my life was I more alive than I was in those few days. I wanted more from him, but he insisted it was for the best that we didn't exchange numbers, and I didn't argue. I knew how busy my life was, and letting him go seemed like the responsible thing to do. But now he's back in my life, and he wants me.

I still don't have time to give him all the attention he deserves, but he was insistent on not wanting a boyfriend because he'll also be busy once the hockey season starts. He wants something purely physical. I want to fight it, but the idea is insanely intriguing.

With the pancakes done and in the oven to keep warm, I head to my kitchen table, where my laptop is, and pull up the policy on faculty dating students. If I'm going to take the plunge with Ben, I have to ensure this doesn't go against the rules before I make up my mind.

CHAPTER NINE

SOMETHING SWEET TICKLES my nose as my body begins to wake, but I groan when I move. *Why do I hurt so bad? And why won't my head stop throbbing?*

Slowly, I open my eyes but instantly shut them when the bright light from the window burns my retinas. Fuck, that hurt like a son of a bitch.

I try to figure out why I'm so tired and in pain, and the memories of last night slowly trickle in. I went to a house party at Parker's and clearly drank too much, if the sharp pain in my skull is any indication.

With much more strength than it should take, I force my eyes open again, blinking several times until my eyes adjust, though they still burn. I don't typically forget to shut my blinds, but considering I was drunk enough to forget a whole hell of a lot, it makes sense I didn't do it when I got home.

Once I'm able to keep my eyes open without the intense burning sensation, I look around. This is not my room.

Where the fuck am I?

It takes me a minute of staring at the unfamiliar space for the memories of the rest of last night to come flooding back.

Fuck.

I sent Ian a bunch of texts, and he picked me up. The alcohol caused me to forget my address, so he brought me to his house. Of course, he was a gentleman and made me take the spare bedroom instead of taking advantage of my drunken state. The half-empty bottle of water and the aspirin container sit on the nightstand as a reminder of how sweet he is for ensuring I was taken care of.

I grab the aspirin and take two more. There is enough water to wash them down but not enough to quench my thirst. I seriously envy people who have never experienced a hangover. This is one of the many reasons I don't drink often.

The same sweet smell that woke me wafts into the room again, and my stomach growls. What did Ian make that smells so delicious?

With heavy limbs, I pick my clothes off the floor and dress myself at a sloth's pace before padding down the hall, following the delicious aroma like it's a trail of breadcrumbs.

"You're alive," Ian states when I walk into the kitchen.

He's sitting at the table grading paperwork with glasses perched on his nose, somehow making him sexier.

"I might be alive, but I feel like death," I grumble.

He chuckles. "I figured you might say something like that. You did drink enough to forget your own address."

Getting up, he heads toward the oven and opens it, causing the sweet smell to grow, which makes my stomach growl some more.

"Are you hungry?" he checks.

I nod. "I'm starving."

"Sit at the table," he instructs. "I'll dish you up some pancakes. Do you want coffee too?"

"Yes, please," I whisper, enjoying him taking care of me. "Black is fine."

He nods, and a small smile spreads across his face as he dishes up a plate for me.

I'm going to bask in his kindness while I can because it won't last for long. Eventually, he's going to restate how we need to keep our distance and send me on my way. At least I'm prepared for it.

"Did you sleep all right?" he asks, setting a plate of pancakes and coffee in front of me. He then takes a seat across from me at the table.

"I think I did," I reply, sipping the delicious, caffeinated bean juice. "I passed out pretty solidly."

Ian chuckles. "I noticed. When I peaked in to check on you this morning, you were dead to the world."

"That doesn't surprise me. It's one of the many reasons I don't get drunk often."

"Could you get in trouble with the hockey team for drinking while being underage?" Ian inquires with a sweet and caring tone.

"If I was still underage, yes," I reply. "But I turned twenty-one two days before classes started."

"Oh," Ian murmurs. "I'm sorry for assuming you would do something reckless like that."

I wave him off. "Don't apologize. It happens more often than it should. Most guys don't think they'll ever get caught. Lots don't, but it was never a risk I was willing to take. I'm kind of a rule follower, for the most part. I respect my team too much to do something stupid that would jeopardize my ability to play."

He smiles, and I'm pretty sure there is a hint of admiration in his eyes. "Are you planning on going pro when you're finished?"

I shake my head. "I've been told I have the potential to make it if I wanted to, but that was never my dream."

"Does your dream have something to do with helping sick kids?" he asks, resting his elbows on the table and leaning toward me.

My brows fly up, and I almost gasp. He remembered our conversation at the resort. When he asked how I would live my life if money weren't an issue, I told him I would make sure that no sick kid ever had to be alone. I saw it too much in the foster care system, and if I could prevent that from happening, I would.

"At first, I considered being a pediatric doctor, but I quickly realized I couldn't handle it if I lost a patient, so I'm going into sports medicine," I tell him, waiting for the common response I normally receive about how challenging it is going to be. Like I'm not already aware of that fact.

"That's awesome," he replies with a genuine grin. "Do you want to work with hockey players or in a different sport?"

"Working for a hockey team would be my first choice, but it would also be cool to work at a university like GSU taking care of a bunch of different athletes," I explain.

I have always found it so cool that GSU has its own team of doctors to take care of its athletes.

"I bet if you put in the right amount of effort, you'll be able to do whatever you want," he says, and his words of encouragement fill my chest with this warm fuzziness.

"Thanks," I whisper, setting my focus on eating my pancakes, which are fucking delicious. It's hard not to moan while I devour them.

"Somebody has a healthy appetite. Would you like some more?" Ian asks when I finish at a rapid speed the three he gave me.

"Yes, please," I reply, even though I'll have to work my ass off in the gym for eating this many carbs, but it will totally be worth it.

"So, I've been thinking about your proposition," Ian states, dishing up my plate with two more pancakes.

"Oh?" I ask, lifting a brow at him.

Has the sexy professor turned over a new leaf? Is he seriously considering being in a friends-with-benefits relationship with me? Because there is no way I'll turn it down if he is.

"I looked into GSU's policy on staff dating students and

found out a relationship between us would be allowed if we fill out the proper paperwork. Since I'm not your professor, there is no way I could affect your grades, and I don't hold a position of power over you. However, in order for the school to avoid any blowback, we still have to disclose our relationship ahead of time. Even if you no longer want any sort of relationship with me, I'm still going to fill out a form alerting the school of our brief history."

A smile slowly spreads across my face. "Are you saying what I think you are?" I check.

He inhales deeply before slowly blowing it out like he's trying to find the strength to say the words. "Like you said the other night, neither of us has the time to devote to a traditional relationship, but you weren't wrong about our needs and desires. So, if you're still on board with it, I'd be open to a friends-with-benefits situation with you, with one clause."

"What's the clause?" I inquire.

"We'll be exclusive," he states firmly. "I'm the jealous type. It wouldn't bode well if I were beating up students for bragging about fucking you."

I snicker, the picture of Ian punching a student in the face popping into my head. I'm unsure why I find it funny, but it's also hot.

"I'll be honest with you. I have a history of being a fuck boy. I've never been exclusive with anyone, but I'm willing to try it. Keep in mind, there is a possibility of people talking about sleeping with me in the past."

"If it's in the past and stays there, I can work with that. I'm just not willing to share you," he tells me, and I respect his honesty.

"I'm not the cheating type," I assure him. I've never been in a relationship, but I've seen enough people get cheated on that I vowed I would never be that person. "So, if you start feeling jealous over rumors or people gossiping, you need to talk to me."

He smiles and dips his chin. "I can do that. I've printed out the paperwork we'll need to sign. Is there a time on Monday that would work for you to drop them off? It would probably be best if we did it together. I doubt there will be any questions right then and there, but if there are, at least we'll both be around to answer them."

"Normally, I sleep in on Mondays, but I could meet you first thing in the morning before your first class."

His face lights up at my response, and I love that I was able to put that look on his face.

"That would be perfect. I still can't believe I'm agreeing to this," he says, shaking his head.

"Are you sure you're okay with it?" I question, and he shrugs.

"Honestly?"

I nod. "It's usually best to go with the truth."

He sighs. "I'm conflicted. On one hand, all I think about is you, and I'd love to fuck you again." His words cause a lustful shiver to run down my spine. "But on the other, I'm battling this ethical side of myself that keeps screaming you're a student."

I reach across the table with my hand out and wait for him to take it. When he does, I squeeze it. "I understand where you're coming from and agree it would be wrong for us to fool around if you were *my* professor, but you're not. We're both adults and are taking the proper steps to inform the school about our relationship so we're in the clear, ethically."

He nods, rubbing his temple with his other hand. "I understand that, but it's going to take a minute to wrap my head around it all. I have never considered dating a student, so it's all new."

I squeeze his hand again. "Take all the time you need. I'll be here waiting when you're ready," I assure him. "Especially now that I know you want me the same way I want you. I'll admit, I went out last night with the mindset of finding someone to hook up with. I was desperate to get over you, but every person who crossed my path felt wrong. I even shot down the puck bunny who was more than willing to go to bed with me. In the past, I would have jumped at the opportunity, but my cock didn't even so much as stir at her flirting. In fact, I almost threw up from the smell of her perfume. All I could think about was wanting to be with you."

Ian's eyebrows shoot up at my confession, and then a look of desire crosses his face. "Your words shouldn't turn me on as much as they do."

"Just admit that fighting whatever this is between us is pointless," I urge him. "I want you, and you want me. Pushing each other away is only going to cause extra stress that neither of us needs."

"You're not wrong," he mutters, making me chuckle.

I slide my half-eaten plate to the side. "Ready to let go of the stress and fuck me already?"

"You're such a fucking brat," he growls out, and I shrug.

"Do you want me to be less?"

He shakes his head. "I don't want you compliant. I'm up for the challenge of taming you in the bedroom."

I smirk at him, pushing my chair back and standing in front of him, still holding his hand. "I'm eager to see you try… *Daddy*."

The title falls so easily from my lips this time, with no hesitation like there was when we first met. I know what I want now, and it's to let Ian dominate me.

He growls again and tugs me onto his lap.

"Before we go any further, we need to have a conversation about consent, and what this dynamic is going to be," he states. "While we were at the resort, things were hot and heavy, but honestly, we should have had this conversation then. Especially when you called me Daddy for the first time, but I'll admit, I was too caught up in my desire for you. I can't let that happen again. Have you ever been in a Dom/sub dynamic?"

I shake my head. "I didn't even know I was submissive before I met you. I've always been the one who took control of all my sexual encounters, but when you took those reins from me this summer, something clicked into place. I've done a fair bit of research since then on kink and stuff. To say my mind was blown with what I discovered would be an understatement. I considered exploring more of that side of myself, but it felt daunting and almost wrong on some level to find someone else to experience that with. I figured one day when I had more free time and felt ready, I'd put forth the effort to look for a Dom, but that wasn't going to be for a while. I read a lot about the importance of vetting, and there is no way, with my busy schedule, that I would have the time to do that. I decided that for the time being, I would push that side of myself down."

He smiles at my response and runs his nose up my neck to my ear. "I'm happy that you've done your research, but since you're a newbie, we really need to have this conversation." I nod and wait for him to continue. "I will only do what you feel comfortable with. We could use safewords, but with how light our kink is right now, you could just say stop or no, and I'll stop whatever I'm doing. I never want you to be uncomfortable."

"I appreciate that, and I'll tell you if things get too much. Right now, I'm really into you taking the lead in the bedroom and calling you Daddy. I liked when you smacked my ass a couple of times while we were on vacation and would be open to a more intense spanking scene. I'm intrigued about experiencing subspace and trying to reach that point. Edging is intense, and I enjoyed that too. The orgasm denials are torture, but I don't hate them. I think that's what I'm comfortable with for now, but if you want to try something new, I might be open to that if we talk about it," I tell him.

"That works for me. Obviously, communication is a huge aspect of kink, so please talk to me if you're ever uncomfortable about something or if you have an idea of something you want to try. I'd love to help you explore anything your heart desires. If you want, we could eventually fill out a kink checklist and find out what new things we want to discover. For now, though, it sounds like we're both on the same page."

I wiggle in his lap with a big grin. "So, are you finally gonna fuck me silly, or do I have to take care of this myself?" I check, palming my cock through my pants.

Ian growls, then whispers into my ear, "Clearly, you've forgotten how things were at the resort. Don't worry, I'll have you being an obedient little boy in no time." He nips at my ear, making my whole body shiver with desire. "And if you're not, then I'll just have to remind you how fond of edging and orgasm denial I am."

I whimper at his words, and my eyes roll into the back of my head when he moves his lips to my neck, sucking a bruise for the world to see. His caveman ways have my cock throbbing in my jeans, wishing I was naked right now.

"I need you," I plead.

Ian chuckles. "You'll have me when I'm good and ready. Just because you were the one pursuing me these past few weeks doesn't mean you're the one in charge now. We both know you don't really want to take the lead. You like it when I take the reins in the bedroom, don't you?"

I nod, but Ian clicks his tongue. "Words, sweet boy. Or did you forget everything I taught you this summer? Do I have to start my lessons all over?"

I shake my head. "No, Daddy. I could never forget everything you taught me."

His smirk is fucking sexy, and it makes me squirm a little with desire.

"Be a good boy and strip," he commands, gently pushing me off his lap.

I do as I'm told without delay because I'm desperate to be fucked right this second. In the future, I might push my luck a little more, but not today, not when I'm this close to getting what I've been desiring for so fucking long.

"Look at you already remembering to listen," he praises while I remove my clothing. "Leave your underwear on."

"Yes, Daddy," I whisper, then await his next instructions.

Ian's eyes roam over my body, and even though I still have my boxers on, I feel naked. Maybe it's because my hard cock is tenting the material, leaving very little to the imagination.

"You are so fucking sexy," he murmurs, taking in the sight of my almost naked body.

His words of praise make my skin tingle.

While he fucks me with his eyes, he slides his sweatpants down, revealing how he isn't wearing any underwear. It causes my mouth to water, but I stay where I'm standing until he crooks his finger at me, and my feet move of their own accord, stepping toward him like a sailor being drawn in by a siren's song.

"Come and get my cock nice and wet," he commands.

Like the eager slut I am, I drop to my knees instantly. The heat in his eyes is evident, and he licks his lips as I position myself between his thick thighs. Once I'm comfortable, I run my nose along his hard shaft, inhaling his scent. A mixture of citrus and musk fills my nose, causing a tiny whimper to escape my lips.

Fuck, he smells good.

Wanting to obey his command but also wanting to tease him, I slowly trail my tongue along his erection, starting from his balls and moving upward at a snail's pace, taking my time to get to his crown.

"You're pushing your luck, boy," he warns, and I can't stop the smirk spreading across my lips.

"What? I'm following your directions to a T," I counter,

giving him another long, slow lick. "I'm getting you wet. You didn't say how quickly I had to do that."

He growls and fists my hair. His grip is firm, and it burns but not in a bad way.

"Do you need me to show you how I like it?" he asks, his voice deep and husky.

"If that's what you want, Daddy," I reply with a mischievous grin.

"Open your lips, pretty boy," he instructs, and I listen eagerly, letting my tongue loll out of my mouth.

With his hand still in my hair, he pushes my head down and thrusts his cock into my mouth. I gag a little when he hits the back of my throat, which makes Ian pause for a moment, then pull out.

"I'm okay," I assure him. "You can gag me."

The deep guttural groan that escapes him has my cock begging for me to grab it, but I refrain because I'm certain I'll be reprimanded if I do.

With my permission, Ian fucks my face with a punishing rhythm, making my jaw sore and dick ache even more. I fucking adore how he's using me.

I slurp his cock and gag each time he hits the back of my throat, causing a trail of saliva and precum to dribble down my chin. The noises he's drawing from me are dirty and hot, but the moans of pleasure that are being pulled from him are even sexier.

"That's enough," he states, sliding out of my mouth.

His hand moves from my hair to my throat, pulling me into his lap again and smashing his lips to mine the instant I'm close enough. I whimper into his mouth as he devours me. "You're such a good fucking boy. What would you like for your reward?" he asks.

How the fuck does he manage to stay so in control and form coherent sentences like that? My brain is fucking mush at the moment. I'm struggling to find a response even though I'm desperate for him to fuck me.

"Your cock," I finally manage to spit out after a few shallow breaths.

"You just had my cock," he reminds me. "Do you want it back in your mouth?"

"No, Daddy. I want it in my ass, please."

He snickers. "I figured that would be your response. Go lay down on my bed. It's the room across from the one you were sleeping in earlier. I'll join in a minute," he instructs, and I immediately rush down the hall.

CHAPTER TEN

THE CLOCK TICKS LOUDLY on the wall as I take a few centering breaths, ensuring I'm in control of my body before I follow Ben to my bed. When I feel like I'm not about to suddenly blow anymore, I head toward my waiting boy.

A smile spreads across my lips when I find Ben waiting patiently. I lean against the doorframe for a moment to take in how stunning he is.

His cock is tenting his boxers, and I'm filled with pride that he didn't take them off, waiting for my instructions. He's such a perfect boy. His eyes are filled with lust as he watches me watching him, but he doesn't rush me to join him.

"Did you touch yourself while you were waiting?" I check, making my way to the bed with steady footsteps, keeping my eyes on Ben the entire time.

"No, Daddy. My cock is yours," he assures me.

I almost get lightheaded from the idea of Ben being only mine. But that's not what this is. He's mine in the bedroom, and for the few stolen hours we'll get here and there, he isn't *actually* mine. He's not my partner, he's just my fuck buddy. That's what we agreed to, and it's what is best for both of us, but there is a small inner part of me that wants more.

"You're such a good boy," I praise, then open the night-stand drawer to grab the lube and a condom, tossing them on the bed, then sit next to Ben. "Are you ready for Daddy to stretch you?"

He bobbles his head quickly. "Please, Daddy. I need you so bad. I can't stop thinking about how good it feels to have you inside me."

"Take your underwear off and flip over," I instruct, picking up the bottle of lube while he listens to my command.

Right now, Ben is eager to listen, desperate for me to fuck him this very second, but I bet his bratty side will be back next time we are together, and it's going to be so much fun when he's challenging me more. This sexy boy has an inner brat who is dying to be sassy and push back, but not now. Not yet, anyway. That day will come, and it's going to be fucking heaven to discipline him, turn his ass a bright shade of red, edge him, and deny his orgasm until he's a blubbering mess, begging to be fucked.

That day will be nothing short of amazing.

I pour a decent amount of lube onto my fingers, and once they're coated, I slide them through the crack of Ben's bubble butt. Now that I'm aware he's a hockey player, his perfect ass makes a lot of sense, the same as how his body is toned to perfection. He clearly puts in a lot of effort to make sure his body is in top shape for his sport, and I respect that. I can't wait to watch him play.

With gentle pressure, I circle my index finger around Ben's pucker a couple of times before sliding it in.

"Gah," Ben cries out, making me smirk.

"That feel good, baby?" I check, and he nods into the pillow.

"So good, Daddy. But your dick is going to be even better."

I snicker. "Patience, boy, or I might take all the time in the world to stretch you."

Ben tilts his head toward me, showing off his pout.

"Please don't, Daddy. I promise I'll be a good boy, but I need you. It's been too long."

Careful not to pull my finger out of him, I move into a lying position by his side and press my lips to his while sliding in a second digit at the same time.

"How often have you been thinking about me?" I question, continuing to stretch his needy hole at the same time.

"Every night," he whispers. "Even before I knew you were the hot new professor. I dreamed about you often, but the dreams became a nightly occurrence after I saw you in your classroom."

I kiss him again, sliding my tongue into his mouth when he gasps at the addition of a third finger. I'm happy we're on the same page about how much we're thinking about each other.

By the time I have a fourth finger inside him, Ben is a whimpering mess, and my cock is throbbing.

"Are you ready?" I ask, slipping my fingers out of him and shucking my sweats off.

"I've been ready forever," he replies as I'm sheathing myself.

I chuckle, then straddle his thick thighs, leaning over his prone body to line myself up with his entrance. I push my hips forward, breaching his hole, and groan at the tightness of his channel. His body is already choking my cock, and we're barely getting started.

"You feel fantastic," I tell him, leaning closer to kiss his shoulder. I'm practically lying on top of him at this moment, but he isn't complaining.

"Fuck," Ben breathes out. "Your cock is so big."

"You love being this full, don't you, sweet boy?"

He whimpers and nods. "Yes, Daddy. I love how much you stretch me."

Once I'm fully inside him, I pepper kisses along his shoulder and neck, giving myself a second to catch my breath. Ben is ridiculously tight right now. Has he not been with anyone else since our time together this summer? It's stupid even to consider something like that because why the hell would he not be sleeping with others?

The mere thought of him only being with me fills me with this headiness. I'm a possessive man, hence why I made the rule about us being exclusive.

"Have you been with anyone else since we met this summer?" I ask, pulling my hips back until my cock almost slips out of him, then slams back into him *hard.*

"No, Daddy," he whimpers, and I repeat the motion.

"Why not?" I question, continuing to fuck him hard and slow.

"I tried to," he admits. "But all of my thoughts have been consumed by you."

My head spins from his confession. I haven't slept with anyone either, but to be honest, that's my normal. I'm not typically the kind of guy who messes around. Sure, I've had my fair share of one-night stands, but deep down, I'm more of a relationship guy. I just haven't had the time to commit to one, which is why Ben's crazy idea intrigued me so much. I don't have to worry about being distant when I'm knee-deep in papers to grade or trying to carve out time to make sure he knows how special he is. We'll get together when we have time, have mind-blowing sex, and then go back to our lives. It's kind of perfect, actually.

"Turn over," I command, pulling out. I want a better angle to nail his prostate and have him seeing stars.

Ben instantly obeys my order, and the second he's in position, I push his knees up and slide back in.

"Yes!" he cries out, his chin tipping up and his back arching when I find his pleasure spot.

"You're such a loud boy, aren't you?" I ask, fucking him with all I have. "Let me hear how loud you can be. Show Daddy how much you love it when he fucks you."

Sweat is dripping down my back while I try to keep up the punishing pace I've set, and with how Ben gets louder and louder, it's obvious he's enjoying every minute of it.

Ben's cock bobs against his stomach, leaving a trail of precum as I hit his prostate over and over again. My thoughts travel back to the fourth time we had sex at the resort, and he came hands-free. I'm tempted to try to make that happen again, but my spine is tingling, which is a telltale sign I won't last much longer. So I grip his dripping cock, running the palm of my hand over the head to collect his precum and start to jack him off.

"Shit. Fuck. Oh my God. I'm going to come," he yells, and I click my tongue at him.

"Did you ask?" I check with him.

"Shit. Shit. Shit," he sputters. "Can… can I please come, Daddy," he begs, squeezing his eyes shut, most likely trying to hold off on shooting his load.

"Yes, sweet boy. Come for Daddy. Cover those perfect abs with your cum," I command, and he instantly lets go.

He shoots his load like a geyser, a decent amount landing on his face, which is impressive. The rest covers his abs and chest in a sweet, sticky layer. As he comes, his channel clamps down around me, pulling me into the euphoric abyss along with him.

I grunt and fill the condom, my head spinning a little from the intense orgasm. Considering I've been jerking off every night to memories of Ben, I shouldn't be coming this hard, but I am. Maybe that's why I'm unable to push the sexy boy out of my head. Sex with him is different than anyone I've ever been with, and now that I've been with him again, I'm going to have a hard time letting him go.

That's not something I'm going to worry about right now. Instead, I'm going to clean up the sexy boy in my bed, let him rest, refuel him, then fuck him until the sun comes up.

CHAPTER ELEVEN

THERE IS an extra pep in my step as I head to the gym, desperately needing to work off the calories I consumed over the weekend. If the team's dietitian got a whiff of how shitty I ate, she'd be reaming me out. I mean, I did, however, partake in a shit ton of cardio, with the way Ian fucked me silly, but that doesn't replace the need to lift weights.

I wiggle my ass a little at the memory of the best weekend I've had in a long fucking time. I'm still a little sore from how well Ian used my body, but I'm not complaining. It's the best kind of sore there is.

Since my brain is now focused on Ian, I text him to let him know I'm thinking about him.

> Me: Every time I move, my ass tingles a little. You know how to fuck a boy so good he doesn't forget about you.

I'm totally going to be reprimanded for being a little bratty, but I don't mind. Maybe next time we get together, he'll spank me. A shiver of lust shoots up my spine from the thought, causing me to squirm a little.

> Professor Daddy: I'm in class. You shouldn't be texting me things like that.

> Me: You shouldn't be texting in class period. Bad Daddy. You should have your phone locked away.

> Professor Daddy: Sounds like someone is searching for a punishment.

> Me: Personally, I prefer funishments. What do you have in mind?

> Professor Daddy: Come over at eight tonight, and I'll show you.

> Me: Sounds perfect! Now stop being bad and get back to work.

I chuckle, shoving my phone back into my pocket. I bet he's flustered right now. Is he flushed from dirty thoughts like I am? Obviously, I'm aware I shouldn't be bothering him when he's at work. He was already reluctant to pursue anything with me, and this has the potential to make him reconsider our relationship, but it's too much fun pushing his buttons to stop myself. I'll have to make sure I keep the teasing to a minimum.

Earlier this morning, Ian and I stopped at the administrative office to drop off our paperwork. The receptionist assured us she would forward it to the proper parties who handle such issues. In the meantime, Ian and I need to keep things quiet, which is fine by us. It's not like we are planning on going on dates or anything.

This is a purely physical relationship with the hint of a friendship, nothing more.

"Hey, Coop," Monster says when I enter the locker room to change into my workout gear.

Monster got his nickname from how massive the guy is. He makes me feel tiny, and I'm not a small guy. Honestly, I don't even know the guy's real name. His last name is Williams, and I only have that information because it's printed on his jersey. He's a baseball player and really good despite his gigantic size, but we've never been close friends.

"'Sup?" I reply with a tilt of my chin.

"Rumor on the street is Stacey's been poking holes in condoms," he informs me.

My brows pull together as I try to figure out who Stacey is and why I'm being told this information. Monster must pick up on my confusion because he throws his head back laughing and gives my shoulder a gentle shove.

"She's the puck bunny who was all over you at Parker's party," he reminds me, and I gasp a little.

"Well, it's a good thing I didn't sleep with her," I murmur.

Monster nods. "I'd steer clear of her and her friends if I were you. They have this weird pregnancy pact going on."

"How do you know this?" I question, leaning against a locker.

"My sister was friends with her but told them they were insane when they came up with the crazy idea that they should all get pregnant at the same time. Apparently, they are crazy enough to think if they're pregnant, they'll be able to lock down the guy who knocked them up. They are mainly targeting guys with professional prospects."

"Why target me then? I have no desire to go pro," I tell him.

"They aren't the brightest crayons in the box. I assume they just see what is written on the websites and go with it. Everyone always talks about how you would be picked up immediately if you applied for the NHL. The girls read what a promising career you could have if you went that route, and the rest is history," he supplies.

"I'm fucking glad I've decided to stop sleeping around," I grumble.

"Oh? Did you get yourself a boyfriend or a girlfriend?" he checks.

"Just a fuck buddy," I correct him. "But we agreed to be exclusive. It kind of works out to be the best thing ever. I don't have to worry about emotions or trying to clear my schedule so my partner feels cared for. I just call my guy up when I'm horny, fuck like bunnies, and go back to my regular life."

"Damn, that sounds awesome. How do I find one of those?" he questions, and I shrug.

"Girls aren't usually into no-strings-attached relation-ships," I say, since he's straight, at least as far as I know. "But there might be someone out there, and I'm just being a misog-ynistic asshole."

Monster laughs. "True story."

"Did you just get here, or were you on your way out?" I check.

"Just arrived," he replies. "I was about to head into the gym when I saw you come in and wanted to give you the warning."

"I appreciate that. Want to work out together? I'm doing arms today and need a spotter."

He smiles and nods. "I'm doing arms too. I'll meet you by the water fountain." With those parting words, he heads out, and I change quickly.

I've always been the kind of guy who has a shit ton of friends. I guess I'm just likable, but most of my friendships aren't deep, like the fact I have no clue what Monster's real name is. I only found out Rio's real name, which is Arthur Leon, when we became roommates.

Maybe I need to focus on building better friendships. I don't want to be known as the guy who had a million friends, but no one shows up at my funeral.

I'm pretty sure the reason I've always kept people at a distance is because I grew up in the foster care system. Letting people in was dangerous because you never knew if they were going to stab you in the back. It was best to keep to myself. Also, caring too much for anyone was a bad idea because there was always the possibility they wouldn't be in your life for long.

Clearly, I have kept that same mentality in college. I'm friendly with everyone, and I say I have lots of friends, but in reality, I don't know anyone well, and they don't know me. But that's something I'm able to change.

Once I'm changed, I meet Monster where he told me he would be. "Dude, what's your real name?" I question, and he laughs.

"It's Isaiah," he replies with a cheesy grin, making my brows pull together.

That is the last name I was expecting him to say. "That name doesn't suit you at all," I reply.

"Why do you think I strictly go by my nickname?" he inquires. "I'm named after my grandfather which is cool, but I never truly identified with the name. I considered changing my name when I turned eighteen, but that would have broken my mom's heart, so I kept it."

"So do girls cry out *'oh, Monster'* when you fuck them?" I check, heading to our first machine.

Monster's cheeks turn bright red, his eyes cast downward, and he nibbles on his lower lip, clearly uncomfortable. "I wouldn't know," he whispers.

My brows shoot straight up. "Are you confessing to being a virgin right now?" I question with a voice so low, hopefully only he can hear it.

He dips his chin, and I almost trip over my own feet. Monster has a reputation for being a player like me, so I'm ridiculously confused by what he just confessed.

"But you talk about fucking girls all the time," I state, and he shrugs.

"Because I want everyone off my back. If they knew I was

a virgin, everyone would either make fun of me or try to set me up with someone," he mumbles, making my heart ache a little for him. "Sometimes, I think something's wrong with me. I've never really wanted to have sex. I'm attracted to girls, but I've never wanted to fuck *anyone.* I don't understand the appeal of sex, which isn't how most guys' brains work."

I put my hand on his shoulder, offering him a warm smile. "You should come over to my place sometime this week. My roommate might understand exactly what you're going through. You're not alone," I assure him.

I don't want to out Rio as demisexual, but I'm pretty sure he'd be open to talking with Monster.

Monster dips his chin. "Thanks, man. Would you mind keeping this between us?"

"Of course. Who you decide to tell is your own business. I'm honored you chose to tell me. So, don't worry, your secret is safe with me. Now, let's shred some iron."

Monster laughs, and I let him take the first round.

How does a guy go an entire year faking something like that? The poor guy must have felt beyond lonely. Well, he doesn't have to feel that way anymore. I'm going to be his friend as best I can. Hopefully, meeting Rio will help him realize that he isn't the only one who doesn't experience things the same way as others.

CHAPTER TWELVE

MY HAND HAS BEEN TWITCHING all day, ever since Ben sent that suggestive text this morning. Then he must have really wanted to push his luck because he sent a sweaty selfie after his workout. He was naked in the picture, but the camera was angled so the photo cut off just above his package. He had his *please-fuck-me* face on, which had me popping an instant boner when I opened the attachment. Thank fuck I was between classes when I checked my phone. I learned quickly from his first text this morning that anything sent by that bratty boy is NSFW content.

I was itching for eight o'clock to roll around, but I was still able to give my students the attention they deserved. This is good because I couldn't continue a relationship with Ben if he became a distraction, even if he's the *best* kind.

When I sit at my kitchen table to grade my student's assignments, I'm surprised at how quickly I'm getting through them. Maybe it's the promise of having my boy over my knee when I'm finished.

The time goes by in a blur, and I'm almost caught off guard when the alarm I set for seven thirty goes off. Holy crap, I'm beyond shocked I finished reading my last student's assignment. A smile spreads across my face at my accomplishment. Maybe having Ben in my life will turn out to be better than I originally planned. I've never graded assignments this quickly in my life, but I knew I wouldn't be able to give Ben my entire focus if the idea of waiting assignments was looming over my head. So when I sat down, I gave them my entire focus.

I'm pretty proud of myself. Now it's time to clean up and get ready for Ben to arrive.

The knock on my door comes at exactly eight o'clock, causing a grin to spread across my face. I take my time walking toward it, not needing Ben to think I'm too eager.

"Hmm, you're on time. So, you *can* listen to directions," I state when I open the door.

"I'm good at listening, Daddy," he replies, walking past me once I step aside to let him in.

I huff out a breath. "I'm not sold on that being the truth. If it were, you wouldn't have sent that tease of a picture."

"Did you not like it?" he whispers, biting his lip. His shoulders are slumped a little, and his spine isn't straight like it usually is when I've caught sight of him in the halls at school with his friends. It's like he's making himself smaller, taking on a more submissive stance, but his eyes are filled with a mischievous glint, showing that even though he enjoys letting me have the dominance when we're together, there is still a fierceness to him that I love. Like I told him before, I don't want him compliant. I want to have to work for his total submission.

"I *loved* it," I correct him. "But good boys don't send pictures like that while Daddy is working. They *especially* don't send dirty texts that make Daddy hard as a fucking rock. Not unless they want a sore ass, of course…" I pause, taking his chin in my hand. "Were you wanting Daddy to spank you?"

Ben nods his head. "Yes, Daddy."

I take a deep inhale, needing to center myself quickly. Hearing that Ben wants me to spank him turns me on more than I ever thought possible. Ever since he told me he wanted to experience a more intense spanking scene, I've been thinking about it a lot. I'd love to make him fly.

I exhale slowly, raising a brow at him. "Maybe I shouldn't spank you if you want it so bad. That sounds more like a reward than a punishment."

Ben pouts, and I bite the inside of my cheek to stop myself from smiling at his cuteness. You wouldn't think someone tall and broad like Ben could pull off being adorable, but he does it. He's the perfect fucking boy.

"Please, Daddy," he begs.

I tilt my head from side to side as if I'm thinking about my answer. I'm definitely going to spank Ben tonight, but I have to teach him a lesson first.

"Take off all your clothes and kneel by the kitchen table," I instruct.

Ben holds eye contact with me for a beat longer than I expected. Is he going to say no? I told him he could if things were too much for him.

"You can say no," I remind him. "But I really think you'll love what I have in mind if you give it a try. You can always change your mind if you find it's not for you.

Ben stays frozen for another couple of seconds, then he purses his lips and heads to the kitchen, following my orders like the good boy he is.

A giant smile breaks across my face once his back is toward me. I know this is all new to him, but I'm beyond proud that he's open to trying. Teasing him while I eat my dinner is going to be so much fun.

I give Ben a few minutes alone before following him into the kitchen. My cock twitches when I find him exactly where I told him to be. His thick and hard shaft points proudly up. I lick my lips, turning away from him and toward my refrigerator.

"I didn't have time to eat before you came over," I explain, opening the door to retrieve a container of leftovers. I place it in the microwave and then return my attention to Ben. "Your punishment will be having to wait until I finish my dinner. You are not allowed to touch me or yourself, but I can touch you. If you're a good boy, I'll bend you over my lap and spank you like you desperately want me to. Remember, you are not allowed to come until I tell you. If you do, I won't spank you. If it becomes too much, tell me, and we'll stop. I won't be mad, I promise. I always want you to be comfortable with whatever we do. Even if you call things off, we can still have sex if that's what you want, but the spanking will have to wait for another day. Do you understand?"

Ben is panting a little, and his cock is already leaking from my words. "Yes, Daddy," he responds, licking his lips.

I adjust myself in my pants and nod, turning my back to him again and focusing on the microwave for a few seconds. While the food is warming, I grab two kitchen towels, fold them a little smaller, and then bring them over to where Ben is patiently waiting for me.

The hardwood of my kitchen flooring will be killer on his knees if I take too long. This isn't a true punishment, so I want him to be more comfortable. He whispers a thank you when I place the towels under his knees and kiss his forehead before returning to the microwave.

Once my dinner is ready, I take it to the table, sitting as close to Ben as possible. I run my fingers over his pec and smirk at the way he shivers. "Such a good boy," I whisper.

I eat, keeping my focus on teasing the sweet, needy boy kneeling at my feet. I start with caresses of his upper body, trailing my fingers over his sensitive nipples, chest, and shoulders. His body shivers with desire at every touch, causing my cock to strain against the restraints of my clothing. When I'm about halfway through my meal, I decide to take things to another level by taking my socks off and running my foot up his thigh. Then, with the slightest amount of pressure, barely a caress, I graze it over his cock, making him whimper. The sound shoots directly to my dick, and I have to adjust myself again. When I pull my foot away, Ben thrusts his hips forward, chasing my touch.

I raise a brow and click my tongue at him. "Stay still, sweet boy, or you won't receive what you desperately desire," I remind him.

He pouts but whispers, "Sorry, Daddy."

"That's okay," I assure him. "It's hard to stay still sometimes, but I'm positive you can be a good boy."

His smile at my words of praise lets me know he's enjoying this moment, even if it is torturous at times.

Ben's needy moans increase as I caress his shaft again, this time applying more pressure. His breathing is rapid, making it hard to focus on eating.

"You're such a needy boy, aren't you?" I question, without removing my foot from his cock. With decent pressure, I slide my foot up and down his length, paying close attention to the way his body shakes with desire.

Ben doesn't respond to my question—not that I need a verbal answer to know the truth, although he still should answer every question I ask, but I'll let it go this time —he's too lost in the sensation he's experiencing to form words.

While I eat my dinner, I pay close attention to Ben, and every time he's about to lose control, I pull my foot back, edging my sweet boy until he's a whimpering mess and crying out with his objection every time I stop touching him.

"I could continue edging you, or I could spank your ass then fuck you so hard you forget your name," I supply.

His lips part with a pant. "The second one, please, Daddy."

I chuckle. "That's what I thought." I push my chair back and pat my lap. "Lay across my knees, put your hands on the floor, and stay still," I instruct.

It's comical how quickly he obeys, almost throwing

himself over my lap. With a gentle hand, I rub his bubble butt, and it's evident how much he desires and needs someone to take control, grab the reins, and give him time to shut off his brain so he only has to worry about obeying his Daddy. I'm the luckiest man alive to be able to be that for him, even if it's only a few shared experiences here and there.

"How many spankings do you think you deserve tonight?" I question, continuing to massage the strong muscles of his ass.

"However many you think I need," he responds, his voice already laced in a dreamy tone.

"We'll go until your ass is a nice bright shade of red," I tell him.

When I bring my hand down firmly on his left cheek, he lets out a breathy moan, causing the corners of my lips to curl upward as I rub the sting away. If just one smack has him moaning, what is he going to be like after I've teased and spanked him until his ass is warm to the touch?

I land another smack on his other cheek, keeping my hand on his skin to let the full impact of the strike sink into his tissue. Much like a golf swing needs the follow-through, a good spank needs that too. I start off firm but not overly hard. I want to warm him up before building the intensity. My favorite part of impact play, especially for pleasure, is the gradual buildup. By the time I'm done with his spanking, I hope he'll have let himself go and gotten the stress relief he needs. I want him to beg for more and a release at the same time. My cock hardens from the thought of how desperate he'll be. His sexy moans and mewls as I spank him have it raging uncomfortably against the confines of my pants.

I land a few more light blows, then trail my finger between his ass cheeks, circling my finger over his pucker. A chuckle escapes past my lips when he wiggles, clearly wanting more than the light pressure I'm applying. "Are you supposed to be moving right now?" I check with a smirk, even though my boy can't see it.

"I'm sorry… it just feels so good," he whines.

"I know it does, and it's going to feel even better, but only if you listen."

Ben audibly huffs out a breath through his nose but stops wiggling like the good boy he is.

"Do you need to stop?" I check, making sure I'm not pushing him too far past his comfort zone.

"No, Daddy, please don't stop," he begs, easing the worry forming in my chest. Ben is still a newbie, and it's my job to protect him. I would hate myself if I pushed him too far because I was wrapped up in my own desire.

I give his ass a couple of quick and slightly harder smacks once he's stilled, then reach between his legs to play with his balls. The needy mewl that leaves his lips causes my cock to throb.

Ben's body presses down on my aching cock, keeping it trapped against the fabric of my underwear. I hate that I can't feel more of Ben's skin against it. As much as I'm desperate to rid myself of these stupid clothes, I refuse to focus on my own needs. I'm not a selfish Dom, and only when Ben's ass is the perfect shade of red will I allow myself to focus on my desires. This moment is about my boy, not me.

With a firm hand, I continue to spank Ben over and over again, keeping a close eye on the boy across my lap, being as attentive as possible.

Time blurs as my palm lands on his ass repeatedly. Eventually, his ass is nice and red, and I decide it's time to change locations.

"Go to my room and lay down on my bed," I command, helping Ben to stand.

He quickly obeys, and I follow at a much slower pace.

When I enter my room, Ben is exactly where I told him to

be, and I smile, beginning to undress. While I strip out of my clothes, I contemplate spanking Ben more or just fucking him.

I love turning his ass the brightest shade of red, and I'm aware he needs more than what I've already given him. Not to mention, my cock is desperate for some attention. I decide to give us both what we need and climb onto the bed, sitting up against the headboard, my cock hard and standing straight up.

"Come over here," I say with a tilt of my head. "Lay face down with your head and shoulders resting on my lap. I'm going to continue to spank your ass, but you're going to bury my cock in your pretty little throat at the same time..." I pause and pay close attention to Ben's reaction, making sure I don't see any hint of hesitation.

He lets out a noise that is somewhere between a moan and a whimper, quickly scrambling into position, clearly not opposed to my command at all. He's about to take me into his mouth, but before he does, I stop him by putting my finger under his chin and raising his face, silently urging him to look into my eyes.

"I'm going to tell you *exactly* what I want and don't want. What I don't want is for you to bob up and down or suck on it. I'm not looking to come in your mouth tonight. What I want is for your mouth and throat to be all warm and wet around my entire shaft. I want the head of my cock buried so deep that each time I spank your ass, your throat reflexively tightens around it."

Ben's eyes sparkle with the fire of his desire. He licks his lips and squirms, rubbing his cock against the bed. Good, my pretty boy is just as excited by this as I am.

"I want the only squeezing to come from your body's reaction to my hand connecting with your ass. Come up for air between strikes whenever you need to breathe, but at no time is my cock to leave your mouth unless it becomes too much. If that happens, I want you to release me and tell me what you're feeling. Do you understand?" I don't want to pull him from the headspace he's currently in, but I also need him to know that he can stop if he needs to.

Ben clears his throat, answering, "Yes, Daddy."

"Good boy," I praise him then dip my chin, silently signaling him to do as he was told. His head immediately positions directly above my hard length, then he opens wide and lowers himself down. At first, it's only the heat of his breath ghosting over my cock. Then my tip hits the back of his throat, where it's warm and slick. I desperately want to thrust up and lodge my cock where I want it, but instead, I refrain, reaching to caress my hand over his firm ass, giving it a tight squeeze.

Ben's lips and mouth lightly surround my length, enveloping most of my shaft in damp warmth. It's good, but still not enough. My boy can do better. I raise my hand and quickly rain down two smacks, one to each cheek. The surprise makes his body jump forward a bit, pushing his mouth down a few more centimeters.

"Come on now, I know you can do better. Take more. Take more of me and get your Daddy's cock down your throat."

With my encouragement, he does exactly that. My cock head slides and wedges farther in as his lips surround my base, pressing against my pelvis. It's fucking exquisite.

"Mmm... fuck... yesss," I let out with a sigh. "You are such a good boy! You're taking your Daddy's dick in your mouth just right," I praise him for doing exactly what I wanted.

"Now to give us both what we want."

I raise my hand and begin laying down smack after smack, spanking in a rhythmic pattern. Ben quickly grasps the sequence, timing his breaths to land in between as needed. My strikes move between sides, landing spread out to cover the entirety of each cheek.

Time loses meaning as we get lost in our feelings and how

in sync and connected we are in this moment. It's surreal—better than anything I have ever experienced or imagined.

His tight throat massages and squeezes my cock each time my hand lands on him. A layer of his spit coats my shaft and continues to run down, spreading over my pelvis. Gathering that slickness from my body and what's still on his lips, I coat two of my fingers. Then I reach between his ass cheeks, circling them around his treasure.

Not wasting any time, I push against his opening, humming in appreciation when both of my fingers slide in easily. "Damn, baby, your hole is begging to be filled."

Ben squirms and wiggles his ass in eagerness, trying to take in more.

"Oh, it's like that, is it? You want my thick cock to stretch your hole the rest of the way rather than my fingers, don't you?" Ben's ass pushes back harder in answer.

"Do you want that, baby? Do you want Daddy to make your ass burn when he takes you hard, uses your little hole, and claims it for his own? But make no mistake, it will be hard and rough. I have been in your mouth far too long to go slow and gentle now. If you need to be stretched more first, I will, but once your mouth is off my dick, it's very quickly going to be pounding your ass. If you need me to stretch you out by hand first, say 'more.' If you want my cock to do it, say 'now.' "

Raising his head just enough to breathe and reply, he gives the answer I suspected he'd choose.

"Now, Daddy."

"Excellent choice," I reply with a wink. "Lay down in the center of the bed on your stomach," I direct, standing once his face is out of my lap.

I gather the supplies and climb over him on the bed until I've straddled his thighs, staring at his perfect red ass displayed for my taking. Ben's body is practically vibrating when I lay my spit-soaked cock between his cheeks, squeezing them tight around my hardness. I thrust a few times, sliding over his pucker and relishing the breathtaking sensation.

We both let out a loud moan at the feeling, but it's not nearly enough. Leaning back, I grab my length and sheath it, unable to wait any longer. "Spread your cheeks for Daddy," I command, and he immediately obeys.

I pour a thick stream of lubricant that lands on his pucker, trailing down his taint. Collecting it with my fingers, I move back up to circle and swirl around his waiting hole. Drizzling even more on my cock, I stroke it to ensure it's completely coated.

He wiggles underneath me, still holding his cheeks wide. "Pleeeaase, Daddy," he practically whines.

"Such a needy boy," I point out. "How badly do you want Daddy's cock?"

"So bad," he whimpers. "I neeed you inside me."

I groan. "I'm just as desperate for you as you are for me, baby boy."

After my warning about taking him hard, I'm almost frantic to be inside him. If Ben's soft mewlings of desire and how he is trying to grind his cock into the bed is anything to go by, he obviously feels the same way. There is a strong possibility he's going to come the second I give him the signal that he's allowed to since he's on the ledge and ready to jump.

Notching the head of my cock at his entrance, I'm barely able to hold myself back from slamming into him as I stretch my body over his, bringing our heads together.

"Ready?" I check, swiveling my hips slightly, my crown teasing his pucker.

"Yes… yes… please, Daddy, hurry!" he begs. "I need you inside me. I need you to make me feel full."

A deep growl bubbles up my chest from his words, and I snap my hips forward, driving into him in one deep thrust.

"Fuck," I grunt out at the same time he keens out a wail of both pleasure and the burn of stretching him. Not to mention the rub and pressure of my body against the hot, tender skin of his freshly reddened ass.

"You're so fucking tight when I take you like this, baby," I growl out.

"Ooohh… shiiit! I'm so full. I love how your cock stretches me. It feels sooo good," he responds breathily.

I claim his mouth with mine, then pull back so I can fuck him exactly like I promised. I slam myself in with a hard, grueling thrust, grinding down before pulling back to do it again. Before long, I'm driving in and out of my boy, making him cry out in pleasure.

I love the sensation of his tight ring sliding up and down my shaft. Like it's trying its hardest to milk the cum out of me. But I'm not ready to let that happen so soon.

Not yet.

"Shit, you have the best little hole, the firmest ass, and the way your channel squeezes my cock so tight when you come makes me see stars. I want to fuck you and use you nonstop. It feels too good to ever stop."

"Yes, Daddy… use me… use your boy!" Ben pants, mewling out between my deep, punishing thrusts.

He's utterly and completely perfect. His desires echoing mine have pushed me right to the edge of my control. Quickly sitting up, I pull his hips with me, wanting to keep us joined. Ben slides back, rising to his knees, while I continue to pound into him. He starts to shift onto all fours, but that's not what I want. Grabbing his hip with one hand, I use the other to push down on his back, wanting a better angle. Understanding what I want, Ben drops his torso to the bed, freeing up my hands to grip harder on each of his hips. Desperation hounds me, and I can't help yanking his ass into me each time I thrust forward.

"Oh fuck, you feel unbelievable, baby boy. Grab your cock

and stroke it while I drill into you. Come for me. Squeeze my cock with your channel. Make me blow my load in your tight ass," I demand through gritted teeth.

With a loud keening moan, he works his cock, coming so hard his entire body shakes. His channel clamps down around me. The stranglehold his body has on my dick draws a curse from my lips as it pulls me in even deeper. It's like the air has been stolen right out of my lungs, and my eyes roll into the back of my head from the pleasure.

I growl and curse loudly when an intense vibration of desire shoots up my spine. My legs tense, causing them to tremble from the force of my orgasm, rendering me useless. When the aftershocks set in, I buck my hips against him, and somehow, I'm still spilling into the condom. By the time I'm done, my breathing is so fucking labored that I'm a little lightheaded.

My body is spent, and I'd love to collapse right now, but I need to take care of my boy first. Slowly, I slide my cock out of him, causing Ben to give out a tiny whimper from the loss and the oversensitivity of his tender flesh.

"Would you like a bath?" I ask, helping him to his feet.

"That sounds amazing," he murmurs. "But could you join me? I'm afraid I'll fall asleep without you by my side."

I snicker, not bothering to mention there's a strong possibility he'll fall asleep anyway, but I like giving him the aftercare he needs. Honestly, I need it too. And if need be, I'm positive I'd be able to carry him, even if he isn't a featherlight little twink.

Grabbing Ben's hand, I guide him into the bathroom and fill the tub. Once a small layer of warm water is in the bottom, I help him inside, cherishing the drunk-like grin he flashes my way.

"I'll be right back," I promise. "Try not to fall asleep."

He chuckles lightly and lifts a shoulder. "I'll see what I can do."

I shake my head, walking back into my room to strip the soiled blanket off the bed, discarding it in a corner. I'll wash it tomorrow, but I want the bed ready for us when we're done with our bath. Grabbing another blanket from the closet, I drape it over the bed before hurrying back to my boy, who appears to be seconds away from falling asleep.

His eyelids are barely open, but his eyes light up when I come into view. "You came back," he murmurs.

"Did you think I wouldn't?" I inquire.

He shrugs but doesn't offer up anything more.

I'm confused by Ben's shock that I came back like I promised. Has someone let him down and caused him not to trust? He just turned twenty-one, but maybe he's had some shitty exes in the past or something. That might be why he became a playboy and suggested we only be fuck buddies. His studies and hockey have a lot to do with things, but I'm curious if there's some deeper reason he isn't ready to share yet.

Since I'm not going to pressure Ben to open up about anything he isn't ready for, I push away the thoughts and grab a container of lavender oil to pour into the tub, then climb in to join my sexy boy, wrapping my arms around his perfect body.

"I wish my apartment had a tub like this," Ben mumbles, relaxing into my embrace, his head resting on my chest. "How do you afford a house like this? Do professors really make that much money?"

"They can when they've been at it for some time," I supply. "On my current salary, I wouldn't normally be able to afford a place like this, but my grandfather left it to me when he passed last year. I was considering selling it since, up until August, I lived in Detroit, but then I received the job offer and was glad I didn't go through with the sale.

"Are you from Michigan?" I question, and he shakes his head.

"Los Angeles."

"Ahh, you must miss the warm weather come winter-time," I guess.

He chuckles. "You have no idea, but being a hockey kid, I've grown accustomed to the cold."

"I can't imagine the hockey scene is large in California."

"It isn't," he replies. "Thankfully, there was a junior team where I lived that had the best coaching staff and didn't care that I was a poor foster kid. But I knew if I wanted to go to a top college and play hockey with the best, I'd have to move. Choosing GSU was easy. Not only is their team ranked highly, but the college is like no other. I wasn't openly bisexual before I moved here, but the environment here helped me feel comfortable being myself."

"How did your parents take you coming out?" I ask.

"I grew up in the foster care system, so I didn't have anyone I had to come out to."

Hmm, that might explain some of the underlying emotions I was picking up on earlier.

"How did you manage to get into hockey?" I inquire.

"When I was eight, one of the families I was placed with liked to offload their kids into whatever free extracurricular activities they could. At the time, a hockey camp offered free spots to underprivileged children. My foster parents quickly signed me and a few of the other kids up. The coach noticed my raw talent immediately and wanted me to succeed. After that, he continued to find the funding so I could play. Even though he wasn't able to foster me, he was honestly the closest thing I ever had to a father.

"Thankfully, when I told him I was bi, he just laughed and said it made perfect sense. Apparently, he saw the crushes I had on boys and girls over the years, but it didn't bother him. He also understood why I waited so long to come out. Sports haven't always been the most welcoming to the queer community. There's still a long way to go in that regard, but

GSU has stepped up to the plate and continues to show that it's easy to be welcoming. The people who need to be shunned are the bigoted assholes, not queer folks."

I smile and kiss his shoulder. "I'm glad you had one person in your corner growing up. I can't imagine being in the foster system was easy."

Ben sighs. "I had it better than most, but you learn to be guarded. It's hard to trust people and let them in when there's a strong possibility they won't be in your life for long. Coach Appleton was the only constant in my life, but even him, I kept at arm's length for the longest time. I was afraid if I let him in, he'd leave just like everyone else did."

"Is Coach Appleton still in your life?" I ask, praying he didn't eventually abandon Ben like the others did.

"He is. We talk at least once a month, but we both have busy lives, so it's hit or miss. Since he's still in California, we don't see each other often, but he's flown out to watch me in the championship finals each year," he shares, easing the worry I was harboring.

Thank God Ben didn't have to experience yet another person leaving him. There isn't anything more to say at this moment, so I just hold him. The pieces are starting to come together, and I'm beginning to understand this boy a little bit more now.

Of course, there are still things I don't know, but I make a silent vow to myself to try and be whatever he needs me to be. I won't be the one who walks away from him.

"What about you? Where are you from? How did you grow up?" Ben asks after a brief pause in the conversation.

"I'm from Detroit. I grew up with an annoying younger sister and some pretty fantastic parents. I have two dads and two moms," I inform him, and he turns to glance at me over his shoulder.

"Like stepparents?" he asks, and I shake my head.

"I have two sets of gay parents. Hank, my dad, and

Charly, my pops, are married, and their best friends are a married lesbian couple. Trinity, who my sister, Katy, and I call MoMo, and Abigale, who we call Mom. When Dad and Pops decided they wanted to have kids, they chose to go the surrogate route but struggled to find the right candidate. Mom and MoMo, being the best friends they are, offered to help. Since Mom is self-employed, she offered to be the surrogate. MoMo, of course, fully supported her. My dads were over the moon at the suggestion. My moms stayed very much involved in my life even though we technically lived with our dads. I guess I started calling Abigale, Mom, and no one had a problem with it, so it just stuck. It never confused Katy and me that we had two dads and two moms. It was just how it was. I just figured I was extra lucky to have that much love."

"You are lucky," Ben whispers, and my heart immediately hurts for him. I guess he senses it because he shakes his head. "Don't feel sorry for me. I'm glad you grew up having that many people to love you. They sound like pretty awesome people."

"They're the best."

We stay in the tub until the water turns cold, and even then, Ben complains about getting out. His pout is adorable, and I have to fight back a chuckle at his cuteness. Once we're out, I wrap a towel around my waist and grab my fluffiest one for Ben, draping it over his shoulders and gently rubbing him, drying his body off the best I can.

"Come on, sweet boy. Let's sleep," I say, pulling him into my room.

"I didn't bring a change of clothes," he grumbles but doesn't fight me.

"I'll set an early alarm so you have plenty of time to go home and change in the morning," I assure him.

That appears to be all the encouragement he needs, climbing into my bed and holding the blankets open so I can join him. My heart beats a little faster at the way he's smiling softly.

It's becoming blatantly obvious that I'm going to fall hard and fast for this boy. I'm just not sure if there is anything I can or even want to do about it.

CHAPTER THIRTEEN

MY BODY IS SWEATING when I wake up. I try to kick off the blankets that are clearly making it too warm but freeze when a deep grumble comes from behind me. Shit, it isn't the blankets causing my body to overheat, it's the fucking furnace of a person holding me.

An almost paralyzing panic rushes up my spine but calms when a familiar voice whispers, "We have another thirty minutes before my alarm is set to go off, go back to sleep."

It's Ian, not some random stranger, not a predator, and not someone who wants to hurt me. I take a few deep breaths, trying to calm myself. Slowly, my heart rate returns to normal.

I've never spent the night with any of my previous hookups. I didn't want people to get the wrong impression.

I never realized the absolute fear and terror that would take over my body when I woke up with someone wrapped around me.

"Are you okay?" Ian asks, sensing something isn't right.

I roll over to rest my head on his chest, kissing him there. "I think so," I reply quietly. "Just had a minor panic attack when my brain was still sleepy. I forgot where I was and who I was with."

"Is that common for you?" he inquires.

"I don't know. I've never spent the night with someone. It

might have something to do with growing up in the foster system." Ian's body stiffens at my words, and I rush to continue, not wanting him to jump to the wrong conclusion. "I was never touched or anything, but kids talk. It wasn't uncommon to hear about foster parents crawling into bed with kids and making them promise not to say anything.

"Some kids considered it better than being beaten or starved, so they never told any other adults. I'm pretty sure it's something all foster kids worry about, even if it hasn't happened to them.

"Since I've never brought a hookup back to my house and haven't slept over with anyone until last night, I didn't realize that fear still lingered deep inside."

Ian kisses the top of my head, and I melt a little, which is way too dangerous for someone like me.

I *cannot* fall for him.

Not ever.

Things might be light, new, and fun right now, but the start of hockey season is right around the corner, and I'm going to be busy as fuck. That's why I came up with the friends-with-benefits scenario. I don't have time for a relationship, and I definitely don't need feelings fucking things up.

I've become an expert at keeping people out of my heart almost my entire life, and I can't stop now. I just have to reinforce my walls a little more and maybe keep things more sexual and less sweet.

"Since I'm awake, I might as well get going," I announce, pulling myself out of his arms and climbing out of the bed.

"Would you like some breakfast before you leave?" Ian asks, but I shake my head.

"Nah, I need to work out this morning. I'll grab something to eat when I'm done," I tell him, searching around the room for my clothes.

"They're still in the kitchen where you undressed," he reminds me, and I rush out of his room to find them.

It doesn't take Ian long to follow me down the hall, still gloriously naked. Just the sight of his sexy body gets me going, and I have to force myself to turn away.

"It's not healthy to work out on an empty stomach," Ian advises, his tone gravelly and firm, making it almost impossible to argue. It's something I recognize as his Daddy voice, and it sends shivers throughout my body.

"I'll grab an orange juice and a protein bar when I stop by my apartment to collect my gym bag," I assure him, needing space. "If I eat too much before hitting the gym, I cramp up."

Ian stares at me like he's trying to figure out what's going on. Does he sense my panic? Not wanting to stick around to find out, I say a quick goodbye and rush out the front door.

Thankfully, my phone and keys are still in my pocket, and I don't have to go back in to collect them.

My brain is insanely frazzled right now, but a good workout will make everything better. I was actually bullshitting Ian when I'd told him I was going to work out, but now it sounds like a solid plan. I've always been able to think more clearly after I've pushed my body to the limit.

When I slide into my shitty car that took every last penny of my savings to buy before I started college, I pull my phone out and send a text to Monster. He told me he always keeps his phone on silent at night and to text him whenever I needed a workout partner or just to hang out.

> Me: Woke up early. Want to work out together?

He doesn't reply right away, which is to be expected. There's a strong possibility he's not even awake. I toss my cell onto the passenger seat and drive to my apartment.

I'm still fidgety when I arrive at my place, but I smile when I check my phone. A response from Monster states he's up and can meet at the gym in twenty minutes.

I enjoy working out alone, but sometimes, it's nice to have a partner. I find I push myself harder when I have someone by my side. It brings out my competitive side but in a good way.

Entering my place, it's quiet. My roommates must still be asleep, which makes sense, considering how early it is. With soft footsteps, I head to my room and pack my gym bag, not bothering to change out of the clothes I'm wearing.

Once my bag is packed, I sneak out, making sure to be extra quiet. Just because I'm awake stupidly early doesn't mean my roommates want to be, and I'd be a dick to disturb their slumber.

"So, why are you awake this early?" I ask Monster as we're entering the changing room at the gym.

"My sister called," he grumbles. "She's the only person whose texts and calls come through at night."

"Is she okay?" I check, changing into my workout gear.

He sighs. "She's fine. Just boy trouble. I guess her boyfriend's cell was buzzing in the middle of the night and woke her up. She isn't a snoop but was concerned it might be an emergency. Apparently, it was vibrating nonstop. Since he was still asleep, she went ahead and checked the messages. That's how she found out he's been cheating on her. She called crying, and I went to pick her up from his place. I was almost home when you texted."

"Damn," I whisper. "That sucks."

He hums his agreement. "I never liked the guy, but it's not like I could tell her that. If I did, she'd say I was being over-protective. Sometimes, you have to find things out the hard way. I mean, had I known he was cheating, I would have said something, but I just figured he was a prick."

I chuckle. "College is full of guys who only think with their peckers."

Monster laughs, slapping my back. "Didn't you used to be one of those guys?" he teases.

I place my hand on my chest and fake a gasp before winking at him. I'm well aware that I have a reputation at this school, but I'm not ashamed of it. "But the difference between myself and guys like your sister's ex is I've always been honest about who I am. I may have been a playboy, but I never hid that fact. I made sure anyone I slept with knew it was just for one night of fun and nothing more. I didn't cheat, and if I knew someone was in a relationship, I steered clear."

Monster nods. "I respect that. Nothing wrong with sleeping around as long as everyone is aware of the fact. It's the lying I can't stand."

"Exactly! Now that she's free of that dipshit, I hope your sister finds someone better."

"Me too," he murmurs as we lock up our stuff and head into the gym.

I'm ready to push my body to the limit, hoping it will help clear my mind and give me clarity about how I was feeling this morning with Ian.

CHAPTER FOURTEEN

IT'S BEEN PRACTICALLY four days since Ben ran from my place, and every day, I've been itching to text him, each day getting worse than the one before. The only reason I haven't is because I've wanted to give him some space.

His confused and afraid expression when he bolted out my front door is burned into my brain. The last thing I want to do is to scare him off even more by being pushy.

I've repeatedly played it all in my head, trying to figure out what happened and what I possibly did wrong. I still don't fully understand, but it was right after a particularly sweet moment between us.

Maybe he's afraid of catching feelings.

I wouldn't be surprised, nor can I say I blame him, not with the way he was brought up. There's a strong chance that he's worried if he lets me in, I'll eventually leave him, too, just like most people have. He doesn't know me well enough yet, but I'm not that kind of guy.

Ben needs time to learn to trust me, and I'm willing to wait. I don't care how long it takes. Even though we've agreed to a no-strings-attached relationship, I'm kind of already falling for him. Clearly, I'm not great at keeping my emotions out of our relationship. I've never had a problem keeping myself in check, at least not with others I have fooled around with. Maybe there's just something different about Ben.

These past four days have dragged on and on. While at the school, I'm able to tune out my thoughts of Ben, at least during my lectures and class time, but the second I'm done, he's back to the forefront of my brain every damn time.

It's like clockwork, the gears ticking over until I'm done having to focus and can return to my growing obsession. I half expect a cuckoo clock bird to pop out of my head and shout, "*Ben time! Ben time! Ben time!*" It's utterly ridiculous, but it's where I'm at.

Thankfully, Friday is finally here, and the second my last class leaves for the day, I sink into my chair and pull out my phone. I need to check on Ben. I've wanted to give him a chance to gather his thoughts, but I'm done waiting.

Me: How was your week?

Ben doesn't respond instantly, not that I thought he would. I just wanted him to know that I'm thinking about him.

How is he going to know I'm here for him if I don't reach out?

Damn, maybe I should have touched base sooner. What if my silence was taken the wrong way? I don't want him to assume I was freaked out by him bolting. I'm worried, obviously, but that doesn't mean I don't want him anymore.

Geesh, since when have I been the type of guy to overthink this much?

I give my head a shake and start to pack up my stuff. It's time to go home. Ben will reach out when he's ready. All there's left to do now is wait.

There is a small bubbling of anxiety coursing through my veins as I make my way home, hoping I made the right decision to give Ben a couple of days to himself.

I'm walking through my front door and my phone buzzes in my pocket, and the worry instantly washes away.

> Sweet Boy: Hey. Sorry for not reaching out sooner. I've been practicing like crazy. Our first game is in like two weeks, and the coaches are pushing our asses.

Maybe Ben hasn't been ignoring me and has, in fact, just been busy. It makes plenty of sense. That's exactly what he told me when he first proposed this plan. We both said we didn't have time for a real relationship and that this would only be about getting our needs met. But just because that's what we agreed to, it doesn't mean I won't still worry about him, especially with the way he left the last time we were together.

> Me: It's all good. I've been busy too. I was just wondering if you wanted to come over tonight.

> Sweet Boy: Sorry. I made plans with my friends tonight.

My heart sinks a little at his message. I was hoping to have him over tonight. I wanted to make sure he's actually okay. It's one thing for him to send a text saying he's fine, and another to see it for myself. But it's also healthy for Ben to have a social life. He is in college, after all.

Has he talked to any of his friends about us? Did he confide in them after he bolted from my place? Are his friends people who will always be there for him, even if he doesn't know it? I hope so because he deserves people like that in his life.

Before I have a chance to reply to his text, another comes in.

Sweet Boy: What are you up to tomorrow?

A giant smile spreads across my face.

Me: I'm free. Want to hang out?

Sweet Boy: If by hang out you mean fuck like bunnies, then yes, I'm in!

I chuckle at his bluntness.

Me: Maybe I'll just tease you all night long instead.

Sweet Boy: You love torturing me, don't you?

Me: Only because I know you secretly love it.

Sweet Boy: Am I that transparent?

Me: Your body isn't very good at lying.

Sweet Boy: I'm going to have to talk with my body about keeping some things on the down-low.

I laugh again, loving how playful he's being. This is what I've missed throughout the week. His sexy text messages during work hours are a distraction and highly inappropriate, but I'd be lying if I said they weren't a turn-on. Who knew I would miss them when they stopped? Not that I'll admit that to Ben, of course. If I did, I'm sure he'd start bombarding me with dirty messages. A few here and there are a treat. Too many, and someone will find out, which would put my job on the line.

Me: I love how responsive your body is.
Don't ever change.

Sweet Boy: I won't.

Sweet Boy: What time should I come over
tomorrow?

I take a moment to figure out what time would be best. I want to give him my complete attention, and I have some chores and grading I'll need to do first.

Me: What about six? I'll cook us dinner.

Dots appear on the screen like he's typing, but they keep disappearing. The longer it takes for him to respond, the more I second-guess inviting him over for dinner. Is there some sort of rule that friends with benefits can't eat together? I mean, if I had it my way, we'd throw out that label and move toward something more, but there is no way Ben's ready for that.

Sweet Boy: Yeah, I could probably make that
work. But just a heads up, I probably
shouldn't spend the night.

My heart aches a little at the message because I loved holding him the other night. But I also understand why he's putting the boundary up.

Me: Sure thing. See you at six?

Sweet Boy: I'll be there.

After his last message comes through, I begin to brainstorm things to cook for us. We shared a few meals at the resort this summer, and I recall how Ben's mouth watered when he found out salmon was on the menu.

That's what I should cook for him.

With the help of Pinterest, I have a few recipes ready and am excited to try them out. I've always been a pretty decent cook, so I'm confident I can pull this off. But I'm also a little nervous that something will happen and I'll mess it up, which would suck since I'm planning on impressing Ben tomorrow, not giving him food poisoning. Not that I've ever given someone food poisoning, but there's a first time for everything. I only pray it doesn't happen tomorrow.

I've also never been a worry wart. I'm always calm and confident in pretty much everything I do. But Ben brings out sides of myself I wasn't even aware existed. That should scare the ever-loving daylights out of me, but it doesn't.

It just proves how much I like him.

Now, I need the patience of a saint until Ben is ready to admit he likes me too.

CHAPTER FIFTEEN

Ben

IT WAS surprising it took Ian so long to text me, but the space was appreciated. I needed some time to collect myself and figure out how I'm going to keep feelings out of my relationship with him. He's a great guy, and at another point in my life, he would be the perfect person to fall for, but the timing is all off.

Even if it was right, I'm not sure if he's on the same page. His caring and sweet side is just a part of him. Even when we were at the resort, he was cuddly and caring after sex. It doesn't mean he likes me more than just a friend, which is why I need to keep my heart locked up or stop what we're doing now. Because eventually, this will come to an end, and I don't need to be a broken mess when it does. The smart move would be ending things now, but I don't want to.

I like being with Ian. And I *love* the way he fucks me. But it's how he looks at me after rearranging my insides that has butterflies erupting in my stomach. He's sweet and caring once he's done being controlling and dominating. I crave both sides of him, which is beyond scary for many reasons—the main being my deep-seated fear of rejection. That's why I need to keep my walls a mile high. The last thing I want is to be the idiot who suggests a no-strings-attached relationship then goes and gets attached.

Our relationship should be strictly physical, which is why

I told him I wouldn't be spending the night. I also should have turned down dinner, but I couldn't bring myself to do that. Maybe I'm setting myself up for failure by spending time with him that isn't just sex, but it's too late to change my mind now. I mean, obviously, I *could*, but I don't want to. We'll have to see how things play out and go from there.

"You look constipated," Rio states, flopping on the couch beside me.

Shit, I guess I've been staring at my phone, lost in thought since I sent the last text to Ian.

"Just thinking," I reply, plastering on a fake smile.

"Abooout?" He drags out the word, singing it, and I chuckle.

"A guy I'm messing around with," I supply, not sure how much I should spill right now.

Rio's brows pull together, and he stares at me like I'm from a foreign planet. "Since when do you spare a second thought about the guys you mess around with?"

I roll my eyes and scoff, acting annoyed, but the corners of my lips turn up. He isn't wrong with his assessment. All the guys I've been with haven't crossed my mind outside of our hookups, but Ian is different, and our dynamic is different from anything I've participated in in the past.

"Are you actually into this person for once?" Rio asks, and I lift my shoulder.

"Maybe," I murmur. "But I'm not supposed to be." Rio seems confused by my answer, so I continue, "Messing around with everyone on campus was getting old, so I asked someone to be friends with benefits. It sounded great in my head. We would fuck each other's brains out without the messiness of *feelings*." I shiver and push my lips out, scrunching up my nose at the end as if the word 'feelings' alone makes me nauseous, which it kind of does. I've never caught them, but I already don't like them.

Understanding appears on Rio's face, and he places his

hand on my shoulder. "You caught some messy feelings, didn't you?"

I sigh and pout, something I've never done before Ian. Rio's brows shoot up a little, and his eyes widen, clearly caught off guard by it.

"Kind of, but I'm sure I'll have them back under control eventually."

"Why don't you ask him to try dating instead if you already like him?" Rio suggests, schooling his expression.

"I don't date," I reply firmly.

"I know you haven't in the past, but if this guy is different, maybe a real relationship wouldn't be such a bad thing."

"He's a great guy, but eventually, he'll leave me," I whisper. "Everyone always does."

Rio squeezes my shoulder, and even though his touch is comforting, it's not one I crave like Ian's.

"Sounds like you have some stuff to work out," Rio says. "Sometimes our pasts fuck with our heads and cause us to think things that aren't necessarily true. Maybe you should take a minute to contemplate your life since you started at GSU and figure out if the statement you just made is really true anymore. People might have abandoned you in the past, but I'm not going anywhere, and you have other friends who are on the same page."

His words hit deep in my chest, making it almost hard to breathe. He isn't right, is he?

I don't have time to dive deep into that train of thought because there is a knock at the door, and Rio rushes to let whoever it is in.

"You must be Monster," Rio greets my friend, and I clammer off the couch to welcome him.

"That's me," Monster replies with a toothy grin.

"I'm Rio. Our other roommate, Bronny, should be home soon."

"Don't tell me the party is already starting without me," Sasha calls out, appearing behind Monster.

"Of course not," I assure him with a smirk. "Who would do something crazy like that?"

Monster and Rio laugh, but Sasha simply nods like it really would be the most insane thing ever.

"Monster, this is Sasha," Rio introduces. "He's a pain in the ass, but he's fun, I guess."

Sasha gasps, placing his hand on his chest. "Rude." He shoots daggers at Rio, then turns his attention to Monster. "Rio's just jealous because I'm super amazing, and he's boring."

Monster chuckles. "I can tell already that you are the farthest thing from boring that there is."

Sasha's eyes sparkle with mischief. "I love that you understand me so quickly. Maybe we'll have some fun a little later." He winks at Monster, making my friend a little uncomfortable.

"Get your paws off the poor boy," Rio scolds Sasha. "Not everyone is instantly DTF like you are."

Sasha looks at Rio and licks his lips. "What about you? You keep pushing me away, but I'm positive I'll break you down one day. We'd have so much fun together." He practically purrs the words, but Rio rolls his eyes.

"In your dreams," Rio murmurs, shutting the door he's still holding open and walking back into the living room.

Sasha's eyes follow my roommate with a hint of longing. Poor guy. He's the world's biggest flirt and also a notorious player like I was, but I know a secret no one else does. I'm just not sure how long I'm going to have to hold onto it.

"We picked up some snacks if you're hungry. Rio will show you where they are," I tell Monster, who rushes off in search of food. You don't get to be his size without a decent appetite.

"Did I go too far there?" Sasha whispers when Monster is out of earshot.

"If you did, Rio would have said something," I assure Sasha. "But when will you admit that you're crushing on him?"

"And ruin my reputation?" Sasha questions. I lift a brow at him, showing that I'm not amused by his response, and he sighs. "What's the point? He's not into me."

"What makes you say that?" I ask. "Have you actually talked to him about it?"

Sasha huffs out a breath but shakes his head. "If he were interested, I would know."

I chuckle and pat him on the shoulder. "Sometimes, people are really good at hiding their true feelings. Have you ever considered acting a little less flirtatious around him? Hitting on other guys in front of him is probably not going to help either," I advise.

"I know," he whines. "But it's my default mode. I've never had a crush like this."

"How about you try being Rio's friend for a while, dial down the flirting a smidge, and see what happens?"

Sasha purses his lips, thinking it through, and eventually shrugs. "I guess I could try it. I mean, what I'm doing now obviously isn't working."

I'm not sure if Sasha is aware Rio is demisexual or not, and it's not my place to say. But if he stands any chance of getting Rio to like him, he needs to cool it by like a hundred.

"What kind of snacks do you have?" Sasha asks after a beat.

I chuckle, tilting my head. "Let's go find out."

When we arrive in the kitchen, Monster and Rio are deep in conversation.

"I just thought I was broken," Monster murmurs.

Rio shakes his head. "I promise you're not."

I clear my throat, alerting the guys we are here in case

they don't want to continue the conversation with Sasha and me present.

"Hey," Monster says with a shy smile. "Rio was just explaining the asexual spectrum."

"Are you ace?" Sasha asks.

Monster tilts his head from side to side. "I'm not actually sure what I am. I just thought I was a little messed up in the head."

"So, I was explaining that there isn't anything wrong with him," Rio steps in. "There's the possibility that he's demisexual like I am, asexual, aceflux, or a bunch of different things. The asexual spectrum is broad, but also, he doesn't need a label if he doesn't want one."

A sense of understanding is visible behind Sasha's eyes as he listens to Rio. Maybe now he'll understand why I suggested he change how he acts toward my roommate if he actually likes him.

"I wish more people talked about this stuff," Monster mumbles.

Rio nods, offering him a comforting smile. "More people probably would if they didn't feel exactly how you're feeling right now. No one wants to admit that they aren't like everyone else, especially when we live in a society that tends to be hypersexual and is all about conforming. There are a few informative forums online if you want to talk with others."

"That would be awesome," Monster says.

"I'm sorry if I made you uncomfortable by hitting on you," Sasha apologizes, but I'm not sure if he's talking to Monster or Rio.

"It's all good," Monster assures him. "I guess I just wasn't expecting it. Most people assume I'm straight. I have never been hit on by a guy. I'm used to turning girls down, not vibrant guys like yourself."

Sasha laughs. "I *am* a bit over the top," he admits. "But I'll tone it down a little for you."

Monster waves him off. "Don't change who you are for me. I like that you're sure of yourself and don't give a fuck what others think. At least that's the way I perceived it."

Sasha beams a little at Monster's praise. "I *am* sure of myself, and I don't give a fuck what others think, but I also respect people. I promise I won't hit on you anymore."

"What about me?" Rio asks with a lifted brow.

"Do you want me to stop flirting with you?" Sasha counters.

Rio doesn't answer but shrugs a shoulder, making Sasha smile.

Hmm, maybe Sasha is growing on Rio already. I'll have to keep an eye on those two. It will be interesting to see what happens.

Bronny shows up around an hour later, and we start our movie marathon.

I'm happy that Rio didn't have a game tonight and could talk with Monster. He's more at ease already, finally figuring out that he isn't the only one who feels the way he does.

Tonight has been so much fun, and for the most part, I've been able to forget about Ian. Of course, that changes once everyone leaves and I'm alone in my room.

When my head hits the pillow and my eyes close, I'm met with the image of piercing blue ones staring back at me.

The man behind those eyes can steal my heart and break it if I'm not careful.

CHAPTER SIXTEEN

Ian

MY ENTIRE HOUSE SMELLS HEAVENLY. Strong wafts of a delicious aroma from the sauce the salmon is baking in fill the space, making my mouth water. Hopefully, it tastes just as good.

Besides the wild salmon, which is in the best marinade ever, I'm making rice pilaf and roasted veggies. Not only is the meal healthy, but it's also full of flavor. Even though this isn't a date, I still want to impress him, so I whipped up two mini chocolate cheesecakes this morning that are currently setting in my refrigerator. Those aren't exactly healthy, but I figure it might be nice for Ben to indulge every so often.

A knock on my door announces Ben's arrival, and I rush to let him in. He's dressed in a tight-fitting black shirt and a nice pair of dark-wash jeans that cling to his thighs. I bet they accentuate his bubble butt in the best possible way.

"You look good enough to eat," I murmur, pulling him in for a kiss that I have to cut off far too soon. "Damn, I want to devour you, but I've made us a nice meal, and I don't want it to burn." Ben chuckles, letting me lead him to the kitchen. "Have a seat, the food is almost done."

Ben inhales deeply through his nose. "It smells delicious," he states.

"Hopefully, it tastes good too," I reply, then cross my

fingers, causing a grin to spread across Ben's face, lighting it up.

"How was hanging out with your friends last night?" I ask, checking on the veggies.

"Really good. We watched a bunch of movies and probably stayed up too late, but they are a bunch of great guys," Ben supplies.

He obviously has some pretty great people in his life, which is fantastic. I'm happy for him. Even if we were dating, I wouldn't want to be Ben's everything. That isn't healthy.

It's important to have people who can see things you can't when you're blinded by lust or love. Friends are the people who help you to pull your head out of your ass when there are red flags you're missing.

Not that I'm a bad guy or anything, but it's still important not to cut yourself off from others when you're with someone. But I guess that doesn't happen when you're with the right person because someone who truly cares for you isn't going to ask you to do something like that.

Once the food is ready, I dish us both up a plate and set Ben's in front of him.

"Holy shit, Ian. You didn't have to go to this kind of trouble," he whispers, making me second-guess my choices.

"It wasn't that troublesome," I assure him. "Besides, I enjoy cooking and trying new things."

He nibbles on his lower lip, staring at his plate. "I love salmon," he says quietly, still not taking a bite.

"I remembered," I tell him. He stares at me with wide eyes, and I grab the back of my neck. "Umm…. did I mess this up?"

Ben shakes his head, blowing out a breath. "No, sorry, I'm just being awkward. I'm not used to being treated like this."

"You deserve it," I assure him.

Ben chuckles, waving his hand. "I really don't, but thanks

for being awesome. I guess I better dig in," he says, taking a bite.

I want to argue with him, but then he lets out a moan that goes straight to my cock.

"This is sooo fucking good," he mumbles around the food. "Any guy would suck your cock if you made them this."

I laugh and almost choke on my bite.

"Does that mean I'm going to have the pleasure of your talented mouth sucking my cock later tonight?" I question with a tilt of my head.

Ben nibbles on his lower lip again, but this time in a more flirtatious way, his nerves seemingly gone for the time being. He bats his lashes and licks his lips, holding eye contact. "That could be arranged."

He's such a minx and well aware of exactly how to flirt to turn me on. But that has never been our issue. Ben is very confident when it comes to his body. Sex is something he loves and is good at. It's feelings and being treated special that he doesn't do well with.

I want to show Ben that not everyone you let in will leave, but only the universe can say what the future has in store for us and if a relationship between us will last forever. This makes starting anything with Ben even more dangerous because I would hate to be the guy who got him to trust only to break his heart.

"If you're a good boy and eat all your food, maybe I'll let you," I respond, keeping things flirty, which is safe territory.

Ben wiggles in his seat but continues to eat.

I love how well he listens. I'm well versed in the kink scene but have never had a boy outside of the bedroom, but it's easy to envision myself being a full-time Daddy to Ben. Or at least more than what we've been experimenting with. Of course, if we went that route, we would need to use a kink checklist, as I mentioned to him when we first started our arrangement.

"You're such a good boy," I praise as he finishes his food, basking in the way he beams at me.

He loves praise, which is something I picked up on immediately. I try to use words of affirmation with him often because it turns me on the way he glows when I do. Obviously, I'm aware he would enjoy it if anyone praised him, but I like to think he's extra into it when the words come from me.

"Would you like dessert now or after I've fucked you?" I ask, clearing the table.

"Wasn't I going to suck your cock?" he counters.

Hmm, does this boy have an oral fixation? He sure likes to have my dick in his mouth whenever we're together. I'll have to test that theory out later. Tonight, I want to bury myself so deep inside him we won't be able to tell where he ends and I begin.

"You can blow me another time," I state, placing the dishes in the sink and walking back over to him. Once I'm standing in front of him, I place my finger under his chin and tilt his face up. "I haven't been able to stop thinking about fucking your perfect ass since the last time you were here. The way you milk my cock when you come is the best thing I've ever experienced. So, answer the question, boy. Do you want dessert first? Or are you ready to have your brains fucked out right now?"

His lips part, and he pants a little, staring into my eyes. "Now, please," he practically begs, and it has my cock straining.

I smirk at him and tilt my head to the side. "Go to my room and prep yourself, but don't you dare touch your cock, and you definitely aren't allowed to come," I command. "I'll join you when the dishes are done."

His eyes light up with lust and need before he rushes down the hall.

I've played with plenty of boys, but none have given me

the high that Ben does. The way he listens to my orders without a fight, unless he's being bratty, fills this void in my soul I wasn't even aware was empty. He's everything I ever wanted. If only he'd let me all the way in.

Maybe I have to hint that I'd be open for more if he was. That way, he doesn't assume I only want him for sex. I'll take this if it's all he's willing to offer, but I'm craving more.

CHAPTER SEVENTEEN

WHEN I FIRST SAW THE meal Ian prepared, it took my breath away and caused my traitorous heart to flutter. For a moment, I wondered if Ian maybe did have feelings for me, which would still be terrifying, but at least we'd both be on the same page.

My brain and heart are definitely not when it comes to Ian. My heart melts whenever he does something sweet or stares at me with adoration, but my brain insists it's safer to stay closed up. Even if Ian did like me, that doesn't mean he'll stay around forever. Shit happens, and even those who promise they'll stay might one day up and leave.

Pushing away the conflicting thoughts, I strip out of my clothes and grab the bottle of lube that Ian keeps in his night-stand, obeying his instructions to prep myself.

My cock is already extremely hard as I lay on the bed and pour lube onto my fingers. I tip my hips and reach between my legs to find my needy pucker, whimpering when my finger presses against it. I love it when Ian stretches me, but there's something insanely hot about being told to do it by myself. I could play with my cock if I wanted to, and Daddy would be none the wiser. But I was told not to, and I want to be the good boy he says I am. I want to see the way he lights up when I tell him that I listened. It's a heady feeling, and I can't wait to hear the words of praise he'll offer.

I'm leaking like a sieve after I slide in a second finger and scissor them, ensuring I'm good and stretched. My dick is already desperate for relief, but I keep my free hand away from it.

By the time I insert a third finger, I'm a whimpering mess, my needy mewls getting increasingly louder. I can only hope Ian hears them and will come and fuck me soon.

I continue to stretch myself and try my hardest to stay away from my prostate since I don't have permission to come yet.

"Fuck that's hot," Ian states when he enters the room, and I turn my head toward him.

"I'm ready for you, Daddy," I breathe out and continue fucking myself with four fingers. "I was a really good boy. I didn't touch myself, and I didn't come."

Ian beams at me and nods. "I see that. I'm so proud of you," he says, and I melt. My brain is too filled with lust at the moment to panic. "I bet it wasn't easy to keep your hands off that needy cock, but you did it because you knew it was what I wanted. That it would feel much better to come with Daddy inside you. Stretching you much wider than those fingers can."

I bobble my head and whimper. "Please fuck me, Daddy. I need you."

"Don't worry, baby. I don't plan on making you wait," he assures me, then begins to strip out of his clothes.

My eyes follow him as he undresses. I keep my fingers inside myself but don't move them, only keeping them there so I don't experience that emptiness yet.

Ian is fast to rid himself of his clothes, sheathing himself just as quickly.

"Give me that hand," he instructs, tapping against my wrist. I begrudgingly pull my fingers out, instantly missing the fullness.

Ian picks up on what I'm internally going through and

strokes my cheek with his hand. "Don't worry, sexy. I'm going to fill you soon. I just want you to stroke my cock with those slick fingers first."

I grip his sheathed shaft, sliding my hand up and down, paying close attention to the way he moans and thrusts when I apply more pressure or press down on his crown.

I want to find out the best ways to make him come undone.

I want to be his best boy ever.

"Enough," Ian bites out after a few strokes. "Are you ready?" he asks, grabbing my hips and pulling me to the edge of the bed.

"Yes, Daddy," I reply. "Sooo fucking ready."

Ian smiles, aligning himself with my entrance, and without giving me another second to think, he slams forward, filling my channel with one solid thrust. My head falls back, and I cry out in pleasure. "Fuck!" I shout while he fucks me hard and fast.

Ian usually likes to tease, holding off my orgasm until he's good and ready, but it's obvious I wasn't the only one who needed a good fucking after five days of nothing. I didn't even play with myself during our time apart because I was sure Ian wouldn't have liked that. Even though he's never specifically stated that I can't, it just felt wrong. Besides, orgasms are better with a partner who knows what he's doing than by yourself. My hand and even a dildo never made me come the way Ian does.

Ian is growling, and sweat drips from his brow in no time. There's a strong possibility he's right on the brink like I am. It doesn't take long before a tingle shoots up my spine, telling me I'm moments away from coming. But Daddy hasn't given me the command to come yet. If my punishment for blowing too soon would be a spanking, I wouldn't even hold back, but I highly doubt it will be something I enjoy.

"I need to come, Daddy," I plead. "I'm so close I can't hold it back much longer."

"Then don't," Ian tells me. "Come for me, sweet boy. Show me how good Daddy's cock is. Let me see how you come from my dick alone."

Ian puts his foot on the bed beside my hip to change up the angle and nail my prostate, which is all it takes to set me off. I come with a roar, coating my stomach and chest with my sticky load.

Ian thrusts, jolting my body from the force, his movements jerky as he chases his climax. When he finally comes, his shout is loud, and he slams into me one more time and then freezes, filling the condom. Randomly, I wish there wasn't a barrier between us, that his load was shooting deep inside my channel.

I've never gone without a condom, even when guys have begged. I refused to take the risk even though I'm on PrEP. Who knows where all the college guys I've fucked have put their dicks? Who's to say they're careful like I am? It wasn't worth getting an STI, so I always had a *no-glove-no-love* policy. But the mental image of Ian's cum trailing down my leg sends a shiver up my spine. You have to trust someone a hell of a lot to make that kind of decision, but I might be starting to get there with Ian.

"You're such a good boy," Ian whispers, slipping out of my used hole. "Can I clean you up in the shower before you leave? I wouldn't be a very good Daddy if I didn't ensure my boy was properly cared for."

I should say no and just grab a cloth to give myself a quick wipe down then run. But instead, I find myself nodding and whispering words I shouldn't say, "I'd really like that."

CHAPTER EIGHTEEN

Ian

THERE'S a war raging behind Ben's eyes as I gently clean his body with lavender-scented bodywash. He's obviously enjoying the care and attention but is also afraid of it at the same time. I hate that this poor boy had to live a life where people constantly left him behind.

"Would it scare you if I told you I want to keep you?" I whisper, carefully running my hand over his cock, cleaning it but not lingering there.

"A little," he replies quietly. "But only because I want that so badly."

"All you have to do is say the word, and I'll never let you go," I promise him.

"I can't," he tells me, his bottom lip slightly trembling.

Quickly, I pull him into my arms, running my soapy hands up and down his back and holding him through his trembles.

"It's okay," I assure him. "I'll wait until you're ready. I'm not going anywhere either way."

Ben slowly pulls back, not enough to remove himself from my hold but enough to peer at my face. He stares into my eyes for a moment, like he's trying to figure out if I'm telling the truth. He doesn't say anything, but eventually, the corners of his lips turn up the smallest amount, and he tips his chin slightly as if accepting it as truth.

We spend the rest of our time in the shower in silence. I almost don't want to let Ben leave when we're finished, but that's what we agreed to.

I silently watch Ben get dressed and feel an ache in my chest when he heads home, leaving me alone in my thoughts. I pray I didn't mess things up tonight. I just couldn't stop myself from letting him know I care for him.

My PHONE BUZZES on my nightstand bright and early Sunday morning. I want to throw it out the window until I see Ben's name lighting up my screen. I hate to admit it, but I was expecting him to freak out again and go several days without reaching out. To say I'm pleasantly surprised to find out that isn't the case would be an understatement.

There are already a bunch of messages from my boy, so I quickly unlock my phone to find out what he has to say. Hopefully, he isn't freaking out and telling me in a text. But as I read the messages, my eyes widen, and I groan when I find out that isn't the case. Along with some dirty messages is a picture that has my dick throbbing.

Ben's hard cock fills my screen, and I grasp my erection firmly. I woke up sporting some morning wood, but the sight of my boy naked and needy has my dick hard as a rock in an instant. I read the messages that came with the image and snicker a little, loving that his bratty side is coming out to play this morning.

> Sweet Boy: What would happen if I touched myself?

> Sweet Boy: I woke up like this, it doesn't feel right to leave myself hanging.

> Sweet Boy: Is it possible to die of blue balls?

> Sweet Boy: You don't want me to die, do you?

I shake my head and type out a response.

> Me: I guess you COULD touch yourself if you really wanted to. But it would be much better if it was me stroking you. Don't you agree?

His reply is instant, and I chuckle.

> Sweet Boy: It would, Daddy, but you're not here… and I'm sooo needy!

I hit an icon in the corner to call Ben instead of typing another response.

"Am I in trouble?" he answers.

"Not at all. I was trying to come up with a way to help with your neediness," I explain.

"Oh?" Ben asks breathlessly.

"Since I'm not there with you, I figured I would tell you what to do over the phone," I state, which has Ben sucking in a breath that brings a smile to my face. "Does that sound like a good plan?"

"Yes, Daddy, that sounds like the perfect plan," he replies, the excitement evident in his tone.

"You'll need to use your hands, so put your phone on speaker," I state.

"I already have my Bluetooth headphones in," he replies.

"Good. I like that no one else can hear what I'm about to say to you. You're already naked, right?" I inquire, wishing my eyes were grazing over his perfect body. I could ask Ben to do a video call, but for some reason, I want him to come from my voice alone this time.

"I am," he assures me.

"Okay, I'm going to instruct you on exactly what to do. You're to obey Daddy's every command, and as always, you are only allowed to come when I say you can. Do you understand?"

"Yes, Daddy," he whimpers out. "Please tell me what to do."

"Run your hand lightly over your chest," I instruct, causing a hum of enjoyment from my obedient boy.

"Good job," I praise because I don't doubt that he isn't doing what I'm telling him to. "Now gently pinch your left nipple."

"Gah," Ben cries out, and I give my cock a slow, firm tug. I'm not trying to come just yet, but I need to take the edge off while I tease my boy.

"How does it feel?" I ask him.

"So good, Daddy," he replies breathlessly.

"Pinch it harder," I command, applying more pressure to my throbbing cock when he cries out with pleasure.

I never knew that hearing my sweet boy like this would be such delicious torture, but it is.

"Good job, baby," I praise, positive he'll be beaming. "Now, keep playing with your nipple, but slide your other hand down your abs."

His moans grow louder as he follows my instructions, and I close my eyes, playing the scene over in my head.

"Now slide that hand over your inner thigh, close to your needy cock, but not touching it yet." He whimpers this time, and I smirk. "You're desperate, aren't you?"

"Yes, Daddy," he replies, sounding needier than I've ever heard him. "I *need* to touch myself."

"You already are," I tease, fully aware of what he really means.

"My cock, Daddy," he pleads. "I need to touch my cock. I need to come so bad it hurts."

"Okay, sweet boy, grab your cock, but don't stroke yourself, just hold it in your hand."

"F-f-fuck," he stammers, listening to my command.

From how fast his breathing is and the way his voice broke when he spoke, I'm concerned that if he starts jacking off now, he'll blow in only seconds, which is the exact opposite of what I want to happen right now. Ideally, I'd love to draw out his orgasm for a good while, but Ben is only going to be able to follow my directions for so long.

He's a good boy, but he's horny and wants to come. Eventually, he'll decide it's not worth it and do what he needs to get his release. Even though I'm not able to make him wait all day, I do want to draw out his orgasm at least a little bit longer.

"Take a deep breath, sweet boy," I instruct. "You need to calm yourself down before I let you glide your fist up and down your needy dick."

Ben does as he's told, like the perfect boy he is, taking a few slow, deep breaths to bring himself off the ledge. It takes a couple of minutes, but his breathing evens out. Finally, it's time to let him have what he's been so desperate for.

"Are you ready to stroke yourself?" I check.

"Yes, Daddy," he responds in a breathy tone that has my cock pulsing in my hand.

"Start at the base and slowly slide your hand up," I instruct, following my directions at the same time.

Ben hums on the other end of the line, bringing a smile to my lips.

"When you reach the top, swipe the palm of your hand over your head and use the precum to make yourself nice and slick."

I fumble for a bottle of lube from my nightstand with my hand that isn't holding my phone and squirt a dollop onto my cock.

"Keep stroking yourself slowly, twisting your hand each

time you get to your crown," I instruct, doing the same to myself. "If I were there right now, I'd suck you into my mouth and swallow your perfect cock down my throat."

"Shittt," Ben hisses out at my dirty words.

"Do you have lube next to you?" I ask, hating that I have to pull him out of the fantasy but wanting him to fuck his hole at the same time.

"Mm-hmm," he murmurs.

"Grab it and pour some onto your fingers," I command.

He's silent while he listens to my words, and I wait patiently for him to ask what to do next.

"Now what?" Ben inquires.

"Touch your needy hole," I command. "If I were there, not only would I be sucking your cock, but I'd also be finger fucking your perfect ass. Slide a finger inside your tight channel but imagine it's my cock."

"Jesus!" Ben cries out.

I picture his head falling back, stroking himself while also pushing his finger deep inside his hole.

"Find your prostate, baby," I instruct.

His needy mewls grow louder as he listens to my words. The sounds go straight to my cock, and even though I'm usually fantastic at holding off my orgasms, I'm getting close to losing it.

"Stroke yourself faster," I demand, almost growling the words out.

Does Ben have any idea how close I am? Is he aware of what he does to me without even being in the same room?

"Slide in a second finger and fuck yourself hard," I instruct, moving my hand up and down my cock faster.

"Shit. Fuck. Shit," Ben babbles, following my instructions. "I'm close. Can I come, Daddy?"

His pleas have me on the verge of release, my balls tingling with the need to explode.

"Yes, sweet boy. Come for Daddy."

The moment he shouts, I do the same. My orgasm hits so hard it steals my breath. My head is spinning as I try to pull some air into my lungs, but it's challenging. I'm not sure how long it takes until I can finally breathe normally again, and it takes even longer for my heart rate to even out. I've never come like that from my own hand.

"Holy shit," Ben whispers, and I chuckle.

"You can say that again," I murmur. "I was worried I was about to die there for a moment."

"Death by orgasm sounds like the best way to go," he replies, and I swear I hear the smile on his face.

"It would be better if I weren't all alone, though," I tell him.

"True. But at least you're on the phone with me. I could call for help so you wouldn't have to decompose in your house for a few days before someone figured out that you've been missing."

I laugh at his insane train of thought. "That's one way to look at it. But I'm also glad I didn't die."

"Me too," Ben replies quietly.

"What are you up to today?" I check with him. Maybe we could spend some time together if he isn't busy.

"Rio signed us up to volunteer somewhere," he replies.

So much for hanging out.

"You don't know where?" I ask, not actually surprised.

As I'm learning more about Ben, I've realized he isn't the most organized person. It has my Daddy urges twitching to help him out. I desperately need to chat with him one of these days to find out if he's interested in taking our relationship in a new direction, but now is not that time.

"I'll figure that out when we arrive. Rio has all the information we need, so that's really all that matters."

I chuckle. "I guess as long as one person knows."

There's a pause in the conversation. It's like we are at a loss for words, but neither wants to say goodbye.

"What were your plans for the day?" Ben inquires, ending the silence.

"I didn't really have any," I reply.

"Would you like to volunteer at some unknown location?" he inquires.

My brows shoot up at the invitation. I was *not* expecting him to ask that. Although it wouldn't be a date, I'd still meet his friends, which is a big step for him. One I'm not going to pass up.

"I'd love to," I assure him. "But if I'm going to be seen in public, I should probably have a shower and wash the cum off my chest and stomach. Text me the time and location."

"I have to shower too. I'll ask Rio for the info and send it over when I have it."

"Sounds good. I'll see you soon."

After Ben says goodbye, I drop my phone beside me on the bed.

I'm so excited to hang out with him outside of the house that it's not even funny.

This is *huge* progress.

I can't wait to see what happens.

CHAPTER NINETEEN

CAN I blame being sex drunk for why I invited Ian to volunteer with Rio and me? If so, that's what I'm going with because I'm still shocked those words tumbled from my lips. Yet I'm not freaking out like I figured I would be. There's actually a small amount of excitement buzzing through my veins about hanging out with Ian outside of our usual environment. That should be terrifying because it means we are slowly moving into a territory outside of friends with benefits, but again, the fear isn't there.

When Ian made the sweet confession about wanting to keep me and being willing to wait until I was ready for more last night, it flipped a switch in me. My brain is still leery and wanting to take things slow, but trust is beginning to form between us. The only way to grow it is by spending more time with Ian and giving him the chance to prove what I mean to him.

When I got home last night, I spent some time thinking about my friendships and the people I've surrounded myself with since arriving at GSU, and I realized that not everyone leaves anymore. At least, not how they used to when I was younger. I've developed friendships here that I'm pretty positive will last a lifetime, and I'm not scared of them leaving. So why should I just automatically assume Ian is going to bolt the first chance he has?

If Ian were the kind of guy to up and leave after he's had his fill, he wouldn't have said the things he did in the shower. He also wouldn't hold me like I'm a cherished treasure.

Obviously, he was hesitant to say those things, but I'm glad he did. It settled a lot of my anxiety because now I'm no longer afraid my feelings for him are one-sided, which also played a part in me inviting him today.

"Where are we volunteering today?" I ask Rio, coming out of my room to find him lounging on the couch.

"The animal shelter on East Street at one," he replies, and I nod, moving to the recliner and sitting down.

"Is it okay if I invite someone to join us?" I question, twiddling my thumbs awkwardly.

I'm a bit nervous for Rio to hang out with Ian, but only because I want my friend to approve of the guy I'm seeing. Ian, being a professor, might make things awkward, but I'm hoping that once Rio sees us together, he will be okay with it.

"The shelter never turns down volunteers on adoption day, but who are you inviting?" he inquires, tilting his head to the side, studying me.

"You know how I told you about that guy I'm messing around with?"

Rio smirks. "The one you caught feelings for?"

I roll my eyes but nod. "Yes," I murmur. "I was talking with him this morning and kind of randomly invited him."

Rio chuckles. "So, after you had phone sex, you wanted to see him in person, but you already had plans with me?"

"Fuck, was I that loud?" I ask.

"Dude, did you actually think you were being quiet? I was wondering if you were filming a porno or something with how loud you were," Rio informs me, and I groan from embarrassment.

"So, are you okay with him tagging along?" I ask once my embarrassment has faded a little.

"Totally. I'm excited to meet the guy who's tamed you,"

Rio says with a devilish grin. "Maybe I'll tell him some hilarious stories about you."

I pick up the Kleenex box sitting on the table beside me and throw it at him. "Don't embarrass me."

Rio laughs, holding up his hands in surrender. "I'm just fucking with you. You obviously like this guy a lot, or you wouldn't have invited him."

I press my lips together and nod. "He's different than anyone I've ever been with. He's special."

Rio gasps. "Damn. This is serious."

I stick my tongue out at him, but maybe he's right. Maybe I'm already falling for Ian.

Shit. I just hope he really is the good guy he says he is.

RIO and I are standing outside the shelter, and my stomach flutters a little when Ian parks his car and walks over to us.

"You're dating the sexy professor?" Rio whisper-shouts before Ian gets too close to hear.

Yeah, I probably should have given Rio that information earlier, but it's too late now.

"Thanks for inviting me," Ian says when he reaches us. His shoulders are pulled back, and he stands with the confident air he always has. "I hope I'm not intruding on your friend time."

Rio shakes his head and smiles at him. "Not at all. The shelter always needs more volunteers. I'm Rio, by the way," he says, sticking his hand out.

Ian shakes my friend's hand. "I'm Ian, but I recognize your face, so I assume you know me as Professor Johnson."

Professor Johnson. Why does the way he just said that have my cock stirring? Maybe I should try calling him that in the bedroom. Although it would probably piss him off since he likes to keep our personal and work lives separate.

Rio nods. "Yeah, I figured out who you were. Is it cool that you two are being seen in public together?" he checks. "Or are you supposed to be having some sort of secret relationship?"

Ian chuckles. "We've already filed the proper paperwork with the school, so we're fine to do whatever we want. We probably shouldn't flaunt our relationship on school grounds, but they aren't able to tell us we can't be seen in public together."

"Oh, that's cool. I guess it makes sense they would have a policy like that, considering how big the school is and how many students and faculty there are. I bet there are a lot of teachers who have dated students over the years."

"I'm not sure of the exact numbers, but it's safe to say Ben and I aren't the first," Ian supplies.

"Okay, now that we have that awkwardness out of the way, let's go help cute animals get adopted," I say, heading to the shelter's front door.

Ian holds it open for Rio and me, making me grin like a lovesick fool, which is completely out of the normal for me, and by the way Rio is fighting a smirk, he noticed.

"Such a gentleman," Rio whispers, and I shove him gently with my shoulder teasingly.

"He's mine, so back off," I reply quietly, making him laugh.

Ian shakes his head with his lips pressed together like he's fighting a grin. I wonder if he thinks we're acting childish, not that I really care.

Once we've filled out the required volunteer paperwork at the front desk, the lady directs us to where we need to go.

"We need two volunteers with the dogs and one with the cats," she informs us, giving us the option to go where we want.

"I love cats," Rio says, and the lady smiles.

"Perfect, follow me," she states, walking away.

"Have fun, you two," Rio says, following the lady.

"I would have been fine with the cats if you wanted to spend time with your friend," Ian assures me, but I shake my head.

"If Rio didn't want to be with the cats, he wouldn't have volunteered. Besides, it's going to be fun hanging out with you for the day while sex is completely off the table."

Ian smiles. "I agree. It will give us time to learn more about each other."

Once the lady is back, she guides us to the puppies or rather, dogs.

"I've always wanted a dog," I tell Ian when the lady leaves, moving to sit on the floor where two adorable furry friends saunter my way and lick my face.

"Me too," Ian replies, also sitting to give a big poodle some belly rubs. "But it just didn't seem fair to get a dog and not be able to give them the love and attention they deserve."

"That's always been my way of thinking too. Maybe one day when I've finished all my schooling and have settled down in my career, I'll adopt one," I state.

"Are you planning on staying in Michigan?" Ian asks, and I shrug.

"I don't have ties anywhere, so I could if someone was hiring, but I could probably find a job anywhere I wanted," I supply.

Ian nods but doesn't respond. Did he want me to say I was staying? Does he see us being together that far in the future?

"But I still have a long way to go before I have to make those kinds of decisions," I add. "I guess I'll have to start thinking more about where I want to spend my life and do my residency after I graduate from medical school, but that's still over four years away."

"What made you choose such a long career path?" Ian asks.

I've been asked a version of this question a million times before, but most people who ask it sound judgmental. It's almost like they don't think I'm smart enough to accomplish what I'm setting out to take on. But Ian seems genuinely curious, and there isn't a hint of animosity in his voice.

"It just felt right. I knew it was going to be hard to achieve, but I wanted to follow my heart."

The way Ian is staring with this awe-filled expression has me squirming a little, but thankfully, the poodle has a plan to break the tension and gets up to lick Ian's face, making us laugh.

"Your breath is disgusting," Ian scolds the poodle, who isn't offended in the least bit and licks his face again. "I was hoping for a French kiss at some point today, but I was hoping it would be from the man I'm seeing, not a furry lady like yourself."

I laugh as Ian talks to the poodle, enjoying our time together. But, of course, now I'm considering what we could get up to when we spend some time alone together later tonight. Mental images of making out and *more* pop into my head, causing my cheeks to heat.

"Get your head out of the gutter," Ian jokingly scolds with a smirk.

"You're the one who brought up French kissing," I remind him.

"Would you like to come over after we're done here?" he asks.

"I'll check with Rio, but that can probably be arranged," I reply.

We spend the rest of the day helping people find the perfect dog while also laughing like crazy and learning new things about each other. By the time the adoption day is over, I'm tired but excited to spend more time with Ian.

It seems crazy that less than a week ago, I was running away from Ian, terrified about developing feelings for him and wanting to create some distance between us, to now, being here and wanting to spend all my free time with him. It's funny how things change so quickly.

CHAPTER TWENTY

Ian

WHEN WE FINISHED at the shelter, Ben went home with Rio to grab a change of clothes in case he wants to spend the night, which I really hope he does. He also wanted to have his car so I didn't have to drive him home at the crack of dawn before I had to be at school. I can't say I blame him.

While I wait for him, I print off a kink checklist Ben and I briefly spoke about when we decided on this arrangement. We really bonded today, and I'm no longer afraid he's going to tuck tail and run at the smallest thing. Even if Ben doesn't want to take our Daddy/boy relationship outside of the bedroom, it will still be good for us to be on the same page. And learning more about each other's limits is never a bad thing.

No sooner do I finish going over everything than there is a knock at my front door, and I go to let Ben in.

"Sorry I took longer than planned," Ben apologizes when I open the door. "Bronny was home, and Rio spilled the beans that you and I are dating…" He pauses at his word choice, his eyes going wide. "I mean, messing around, fuck buddies, friends with benefits, whatever this is." Ben's words are rushed, and I place my hand on his shoulder to try and calm him.

"We should sit down and talk," I offer. Unfortunately, my words don't soothe him like I hoped they would, but he nods and follows me to the living room. "This isn't the bad kind of talk," I assure him once we're sitting. "I was hoping we could discuss what we both want from this relationship. I know we agreed to something casual when we started, but I also think it's safe to say that feelings are getting involved, and maybe that label doesn't fit us so well anymore."

"Yeah, that's safe to say," Ben repeats my words quietly.

"Where is your head at on all of this?" I ask, wanting him to take the lead.

"I've been nervous about bringing up feelings because, at first, I thought they were one-sided, but then last night, you hinted at wanting more, which settled some of my anxiety. I've never actually dated anyone. I'm not sure if I'll be good at it, but I'm willing to try if you are."

I beam at him, taking his hand in mine. "You're going to do just fine, but like I said when we first started messing around, it's important to keep conversations open and talk about what we're feeling. If you're ever worried about anything, please come to me. I won't be able to fix something I'm not aware is broken."

Ben's face lights up at my words. "That sounds perfect."

"Now that we have that part settled, I was also curious how you felt about our Daddy/boy relationship," I inquire. "Did you want to keep it strictly to the bedroom or would you like it if I took more control of your day-to-day life as well?"

"What would that look like?" he inquires.

"Whatever you want it to." I reach over and grab the papers I printed and the pens I already set out. "Let's start by filling these in and figure out where we are at this moment, then go from there." Ben eyes the papers but doesn't seem to be taken off guard. He probably saw a version of a kink checklist when he was doing his research. "It's a standard form, and there are no right or wrong answers. I promise, no matter what, I'll still want to be with you. This is only to figure out if there are ways I can better satisfy you. If you have any questions, feel free to ask them at any time."

Ben smiles and starts to fill out his form. I do the same, working a little faster since I'm more aware of my likes and dislikes and have filled out a form like this in the past. I pause anytime my sweet boy has a question, then get back to work. Besides the occasional question here and there, we are silent, but it's not uncomfortable. It's actually calming. I like having Ben beside me like this.

"Okay, done," Ben says, handing over his papers. I do the same so he can read mine.

"Would you like to go over them together, or would you like to read mine silently first?" I ask him.

"Together, please," Ben replies. "I'm afraid if I go over it silently, I'll get all up in my head about stuff."

"Thank you for telling me that. See? You're already a pro at the communication part," I praise him and start reading over our responses.

I'm not sure why I am surprised at just how compatible we are, but I am, in a good way, of course. We agree to use the traffic light system as our safewords even though neither of us is into hard-core kinks, but it never hurts to have that in place. What makes me the most excited is Ben being open to handing over more control of his life. He wants to keep things small and simple to begin with to see how he feels about it, which is the perfect idea.

"How about we start by you reaching out anytime there is a decision to be made? Not for me to make it for you, but so I'm able to help you come up with your answer. I'd also like to help you pick out your outfits each day, and I want to do daily check-ins to ensure you're eating regularly. My last rule would be, I want you to watch your mouth and curb your swearing when I'm around. Because good boys don't curse like sailors," I explain. "Does that sound good to you?"

Ben nods with a big smile. "The no swearing is going to

suck, but the rest sounds perfect. I hate picking what I'm going to wear, and big decisions make my skin crawl."

I chuckle. "Sounds like you've needed a Daddy all along."

Ben blushes, tilting his head from side to side. "Maybe, but I'm glad it's you."

I grab his chin and lean in. "Me too," I whisper, bringing him in for a passionate kiss.

My tongue dances along the seam of his lips until he parts them, giving access to his warm mouth for mine to play with his. Tiny moans break free from Ben as we make out, and I grip his hips, guiding him to straddle me.

"I've been thinking about something," Ben whispers when we take a pause for some air.

"What's that, handsome?" I ask, nipping at his neck.

"When we were going over the sheets, we both said the only bodily fluids we were open to was cum, but it didn't mention in what manner. Like obviously, we've both given blow jobs to each other, but what would you think about getting tested and going without condoms?" he inquires. "I've always used condoms with any guy I've been with in the past, and I'm on PrEP. I just keep having these dirty daydreams about you breeding me. It seriously gets me all hot and bothered."

The idea of filling him with my load has popped into my mind before, but I wasn't sure when would be the right time to bring it up. Now that Ben's talking about it, I'm one hundred percent on board.

"That's a big step," I reply, wanting to just say yes and book an appointment at the clinic, but knowing I need to make sure this is the right move for us. "Are you sure you're ready for that?"

Ben nibbles on his lower lip. There is a hint of doubt behind his eyes, which is what I was worried about.

"I'd love to be bare with you, baby," I assure him, making sure he doesn't just assume I'm saying this because I don't want to experience this with him. "But I need to be sure you aren't making this decision impulsively. How about we book appointments for testing but still think about it for a little bit before we take the plunge."

Ben's eyes glimmer as he nods. "I like that idea."

I grin, then kiss him again. "Daddies are usually pretty good at coming up with solutions to things."

Ben chuckles. "I'm glad I have you."

"I'm not going anywhere," I assure him. "I like you a lot, and I'm excited to see where things go with us."

"Me too," my sweet boy whispers. "Now take me to bed and fuck me silly, Daddy."

I raise a brow at him and click my tongue. "Did you forget my rule already? You need to watch that mouth."

"What happens if I don't?" he checks with a breathy voice.

"I'll punish you, and not something fun like spanking either," I tell him, and he pouts.

"Well, that sucks."

I laugh and shrug. "Before we head to the bedroom, we're going to eat. Do you want to help cook or stay in here and watch some TV?"

"I'm not very good at cooking, but maybe you can teach me," he suggests.

"Absolutely," I reply with a smile, grabbing his hand and guiding him to the kitchen.

Today has turned out to be one of the best days of my life. Ben is officially mine, and I can't wait to find out where life takes us.

CHAPTER TWENTY-ONE

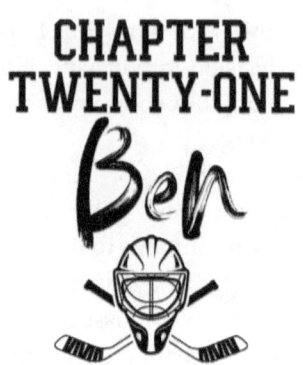

IT'S BEEN two weeks since Ian and I made things official, and life has been great. We don't see each other every day, which I expected, but we don't go a day without talking, whether it be texting or talking on the phone.

Communication is everything to Ian, and it has been key in making me feel safe. I've also really enjoyed how he's seamlessly started to take more control over my life. It lifted a weight off my shoulders I had no idea I was carrying.

Tonight is the GSU Koalas' first hockey game of the season and the energy humming through my veins as I stand in front of the net is something I've always loved. I understand why people would want to go professional and chase this high all the time. It's like nothing I've ever experienced.

I cast a quick glance at the stands, taking a swig of my water and trying to find Ian. I'm fucking ecstatic that he is here tonight to cheer us on. It only makes things better. I want to play the best game I've ever played because of him. I want to make him proud.

Once the puck is dropped, my head is back in the game, trying my hardest not to let a single puck enter my net. It's not often we get shutouts since we play some extremely talented teams, but it's still my goal for tonight.

The score is currently two-zero for us, and I plan on keeping that zero in place until the buzzer sounds at the end.

The game goes by in a blur like they usually do, and when I glance up at the final score, I am smiling. We got the shutout and ended up winning the game with a score of four-zero.

"Way to start off the season, boys," Coach Wynter tells us when we enter the locker room. "We have a long road ahead of us, but I have faith that we'll bring home the championship again this year. Now, hit the showers and make sure you're taking care of your bodies. If you need to see any of the trainers, do it. We don't need any of you trying to be tough guys and getting injured for a reason that could have been avoided."

"Yes, Coach," we all shout, then move to shower and change into clean clothes.

I'm exhausted when I pull up to Ian's house but also excited to find out what he thought about the game. Did I make him proud? Did he enjoy himself?

My hands shake as I lift my fist to knock on his door. Ian will most likely tell me I did good, but it doesn't stop the nervous energy from coursing through my veins.

I'm not entirely sure why I'm anxious right now, probably because it was the first time my man has seen me play. I have people telling me how talented I am all the time, but their words don't mean anything to me. Ian's words do.

When my sexy professor opens the door, he's in a pair of gray sweats that are sitting low on his hips, and he isn't wearing a shirt. His hair is damp, and a few water droplets cling to his chest. He must have just gotten out of the shower.

I lick my lips, and Ian smirks. "Enjoying the view?" he asks, and I shift my head to the side.

"What's not to like?" I reply. "Would it be okay if I had a taste?"

He inhales deeply through his nose before lifting his chin, inviting me into his house. "What exactly do you want to taste?" he questions, walking into his living room and sitting on the couch.

My cock is instantly hard from the deep timbre of his voice. His Daddy voice instantly sends shivers of lust down my spine, and I'm eager to obey.

Of course, my bratty side likes to come out occasionally, but what fun would things be if I didn't keep him on his toes?

"Everything," I whisper breathily.

Ian spreads his knees and then crooks his finger. I rush to obey him, and the second I'm in front of him, he commands me to kneel. When I don't instantly drop to my knees, Ian lifts a brow at me, and it's like he's saying, "*Do you want to challenge me right now, boy?*"

I contemplate pushing my luck for a moment but then think better of it, sinking to my knees between his thighs. I want to suck his cock so bad it hurts, and if I don't listen, it's going to be a long time before I get what I want, possibly even longer until he allows me to come.

"Good boy," he praises, leaning down to kiss my lips. "I loved watching you play tonight. You're so incredibly skilled at what you do... so powerful and in control. It makes having you on your knees even more of a prize for me. I'm such a lucky guy to have you."

My heart beats rapidly at his sweet words, making it hard to breathe. I thought I was lucky to have a man like Ian in my life, and here he is saying it's him. It is almost mind-boggling.

Thankfully, I don't have much time to overthink things because Daddy is kissing me. His tongue dives into my eager mouth, and I moan. This man knows exactly how to take control of a kiss, which is a huge turn-on. He devours my mouth and swallows my needy whimpers.

He'll only release me once he's had his fill. That's how everything with Ian is. He takes the reins, and things move at his pace. I never knew I would be this into someone taking the amount of control he does, but I am. I crave the ability to just let go. The only thing I have to worry about when I'm with Ian is listening to him—he's in charge of the rest. I love it.

"You taste fucking delicious, baby," Ian says.

"Thank you, Daddy," I reply. "Can I taste more of you?"

Ian leans back, spreading his arms open and resting them on the couch. "I mean, you definitely deserve a prize for how amazing you played tonight. Where did you want to taste?" he inquires.

I lick my lips. "Everywhere."

"Okay," he responds with a devilish grin. "Any exposed skin is fair game. Show me how talented your mouth is."

"May I sit in your lap to start?" I request.

Ian nods, and I scramble into position, straddling him quickly. A deep chuckle reverberates through his chest, making tingles erupt just under my skin.

There's a smile on my lips as I stick my tongue out and lap at Ian's neck. I begin at the base and work my way toward his ear, pulling his lobe into my mouth. My lips curve up even more when Ian lets out a low groan.

Letting go, I work my way down his neck, leaving a trail of licks and kisses as I make my way to his pecs. When I stare at him, I almost get a little lightheaded from how intensely he's watching me. He's looking at me like I'm a prized treasure, filling me with warmth and fuzziness.

"Your body is exquisite," I tell him, pulling his nipple into my mouth and giving it a good suck, then biting it.

Ian hisses, but when I cast a glance back at him, his one brow is raised, and the intimate look that was there earlier is replaced with his usual Daddy seriousness.

"Good boys don't bite," he warns, and I shrug, letting go.

"Being good all the time is boring," I reply, then give his other one a quick nibble.

"If you want my cock in your ass tonight, you better start listening," he warns.

I give a long, slow lick of his chest before climbing off his lap and kneeling between his legs again. "Maybe I don't want that," I counter. "Maybe I just want you to fill my mouth with your load."

My fingers dance along the waistband of his sweats, and a deep growl bubbles up his chest, which has my cock throbbing in my pants.

"Can I please have your cock, Daddy?" I plead and am pleasantly surprised when he lifts his hips to shove his sweats down.

Instead of letting me take him into my mouth, the moment his pants are off, he hooks his hands under my armpits and pulls me up. Then he places me on the couch beside him, standing as soon as I'm situated. His thick cock hangs heavy in front of my face, and I'm not too proud to admit I'm drooling a little.

"You can have me, but only what I give you," he instructs. "So, stay still, hands on your thighs, and open that cock-hungry mouth."

A lustful energy dances through my veins, and I obey his command at lightning speed.

"I'm going to fuck your face," he informs me. "If it becomes too much, tap my leg."

"Yes, Daddy," I reply then open my mouth, waiting for my reward.

Ian blows out a breath and then taps his crown against my tongue. Drool dribbles down my chin, but I don't dare close my mouth. I haven't been told to do that yet, and if I want the prize of my man's load, I have to listen.

"Such a good boy," Ian praises, his voice gravelly and deep with desire.

I never knew I had a praise kink until I met Ian, but there's no denying now that I one hundred percent do. His words fill my chest with a warmth I've never experienced. It's something I could easily become addicted to.

He swipes his cock across my tongue a couple of times, his

precum coating it, making me desperate to swallow the delicious taste, but I still refrain.

I want to be a good boy.

"Suck my cock, boy," he instructs, and I eagerly do just that.

My eyes almost roll into the back of my head when I swallow his salty sweetness, but it's not enough.

I need more.

I've always been a bit of a cum slut who loves giving head, but with Ian, it's worse. If I could live with his cock in my mouth, I'd be a happy man. I'm desperate for his load, and I'll do anything to receive it.

Ian places his hands on the back of my head, pushing forward until my nose is buried in his pubes. I gag a little around him, but he doesn't let go. Instead, he holds me there, with his cock lodged in my throat, cutting off my ability to breathe. When he finally pulls back, I suck in a deep breath through my nose, cherishing the precious air before he thrusts deep again.

Some people might not like being used like this, but I find it pure bliss. I get to be Daddy's fuck toy, *and* he only wants *me*. It's such a rush.

It doesn't take long for Ian to forget the idea of going slow, deciding that hard and fast is how he wants it. He abuses my throat, fucking my face with everything he has like it's his job, and I sit here taking it like the good boy I am. I dig my fingers into my thighs to stop myself from reaching out to touch him, waiting for his command to tell me I can move.

Some people might think how Ian is using me is purely for his pleasure, but it's not. I'm beyond turned-on right now, and my cock is impossibly hard. Could I possibly come without even being touched? A part of me thinks if Ian gave the word, I'd erupt like a geyser.

The sweet and salty flavor of Ian's precum grows stronger, and by the way he's grunting, his brows pulled together in an almost pain-filled way, I'm positive he's going to come at any moment. But when he pulls out and steps away, I'm shocked and left wanting.

Ian doesn't say anything right away. His eyes are shut, and his breathing is labored. If I had to put my money on it, he's trying to calm himself down. Clearly, I haven't earned his load yet.

"You have the most talented mouth ever. I almost wasn't able to stop myself," Ian states after about a minute goes by, finally looking at me again.

"You didn't have to stop," I reply. "I wanted your milk."

Ian smirks, tilting his head to the side. "Is that right?" he asks, and I nod rapidly. "And what gave you the idea that you're the one who decides where I shoot my load?"

I pout, staring at the floor. "I was just hoping," I murmur.

Ian chuckles and reaches for my chin, tipping my head up to look at him. "I'm well aware that you wanted your sweet little mouth filled with my hot cum, and even though I'd love that, I've also been dreaming about being buried in that tight ass of yours. So, strip and ride me," he commands, sitting on the couch beside me.

My cock pushes against my clothes from his dirty words. Fuck, I love it when he talks like that. Wanting to obey him right this very second, I stand quickly, getting a little light-headed in the process, but I don't let it slow me down. I'm a little clumsy as I strip out of my clothes, desperate to have his cock inside me *now*. Once I'm naked, I strut over to Ian and wait for further instructions.

"Lay over my lap. I'm going to stretch you," he instructs.

Getting into position, my eyes land on a bottle of lube that is now sitting on the couch with a condom beside it. Ian must have had them stashed in one of the end tables. There's something about a man who is prepared. It's fucking hot.

"Next time you come over, you should wear a butt plug.

That way, I don't have to stretch you," he states, and I wiggle a little at the idea.

Fuck, it would be insanely hot to be plugged while Ian fucked my face. Then he could spin me around, pull out the plug, and immediately sink into my already-prepped ass. It would be even hotter if he went without the condom and filled me with his load. Maybe he would even put the plug back in when he was done, forcing his release to stay inside my channel until he said it was time for it to come out.

It ended up taking us a little longer to get tested than he had planned, but we should have our results back next week. I'm praying Ian is ready to go bare by then because it's literally all I can think about.

I wiggle again, my throbbing cock rubbing against Ian's thigh. *Shit, that feels good.* Even though I shouldn't, I move again, practically grinding against his thigh.

"Do you want me to fuck you?" Ian asks, rubbing my ass with his large hand.

"Please, Daddy. I need you," I beg, and there isn't a single ounce of shame at how desperate my voice is.

"Then stay still," he commands in his Daddy voice, and I immediately stop. "There's my good boy," he praises, rubbing an already slicked finger around my pucker.

When the hell did he lube it up? Clearly, I was too far in my head, lost in the fantasy of Ian breeding me to notice.

I moan when he slips his first digit inside, wiggling it around and getting me ready to take his fat dick.

"You're so responsive and loud," Ian notes. "Don't ever fucking stop."

My cheeks heat, and the corners of my lips turn up. I'm glad he enjoys how vocal I am because it's not something I can change. I've had guys in the past who hated it, but I told them to either deal with it or fuck off. Obviously, they never fucked off. My ass is just too good to pass up.

"Yesss," I hiss out when a second finger joins the first.

It's taking all my strength not to grind against Ian's lap, but I want his cock inside me, and it won't happen if I'm naughty. I pray he isn't planning on being slow with his stretching because I'm not sure how long I can resist.

"Jesus," I cry out when Ian presses against my prostate.

"You like that?" he questions with a smile in his voice.

I huff out an annoyed breath. "You know I do. But you also know that I like your cock even better, so please hurry up and fuck me already," I beg, which of course, only makes Ian laugh.

"Such a naughty boy, forgetting his rules and thinking he's in charge. You'll receive my cock when I'm good and ready, not a moment sooner. And if you don't watch that mouth of yours, you'll be waiting a lot longer."

I pout, even though my face isn't visible to him. Waiting is the part I hate the most, even though the orgasms that result from it are mind-blowing. It will be worth it in the end, but during is fucking torture.

To my delight, Ian doesn't make me wait too much longer, tapping my thigh and telling me to straddle him.

"Face away from me," Ian instructs as I sit up.

I listen eagerly, straddling his lap, then slowly lowering myself onto his perfect cock. The loudest moan slips past my lips when he breaches my hole and slowly slides in. It's about fucking time. Yes, I wanted to suck him dry earlier, but like always, Ian was right—this is what I actually needed.

"That's it," Ian encourages. One of his hands is on my hip and the other pushes gently on my spine, forcing me to lean forward. "Look at that greedy little hole swallowing my cock. Bet you feel so fucking full right now, don't you?"

My head bobbles up and down. "Yes, Daddy," I whine. "So full but sooo good."

Ian snickers, then thrusts his hips upward while shoving me down at the same time, completely impaling my body on his dick.

"Fuck," I cry out, gasping for air. Thankfully, Ian doesn't scold my potty mouth this time.

"Time to ride my cock, sweet boy," he whispers. "Milk me dry."

"Yes, Daddy," I whisper, moving up and down with ease thanks to my well-trained thighs. I could squat and bounce for hours if I wanted to, and I'm beyond excited to put my goalie skills to use and show my man just how talented I am at riding his cock. Ian lets me take the lead at first, allowing me to fuck him like my life depends on it. I'm desperate to finally be able to come, and I'll do anything to earn that reward.

"You're exceptionally hot when you're riding me," Ian states, running his hand up and down my spine. "You're my perfect boy, aren't you?"

"Yes, Daddy," I respond, my voice shaky. I'm extremely close to coming, I can almost taste it.

Ian must notice because he takes charge, commanding me to hover my ass high enough so he can fuck into me before pulling me so my back rests against his chest. He wraps one hand around my throat, not choking, just holding me, but it's one of the hottest things I have ever experienced. His other fist grips my cock as he bucks into me with all of his strength.

"Come, sweet boy," he demands, and I instantly blow.

A lewd moan escapes my lips, and my head falls back, resting on his shoulder while he continues to fuck me. My body is vibrating as my orgasm takes over, and I shoot hot ropes of cum over my stomach.

It doesn't take Ian long to reach his climax, letting out a loud shout, stilling, and filling the condom with his release. Again, the idea of him filling *me* flutters through my head.

Hopefully, that fantasy will soon become a reality.

CHAPTER TWENTY-TWO

Ian

IT'S BEEN one month since Ben and I officially started dating. To say things have been going astonishingly well would be an understatement. I've never been in a relationship that was this right.

Why was I so resistant to starting one in the first place?

Sure, there are days that one or both of us are busy, and we aren't able to hang out with each other, but that hasn't stopped us from being there for the other. I'm not being neglected in the relationship, nor do I feel like I am dropping the ball on Ben's needs. And I'm pretty sure Ben feels the same way.

The only thing I realized a couple of days ago was we've yet to go on an actual date. To be honest, it slipped my brain. Maybe it's because of how our relationship started. When we were fuck buddies, dates were off the table, but when we agreed to be more, we kind of just fell into a comfortable routine. Plus, we're both extremely busy. But that doesn't make it right. Ben deserves to be taken out and not treated like a dirty little secret.

When I told Ben we were going on a date tonight and to come over as soon as he was done practice, his face lit up, which told me I should have done this sooner.

Better late than never.

Tuesdays aren't the ideal night for a date, but it was the

only night this week that worked best for us. I'll just have to deal with being tired in the morning. Although, if Ben spends the night like he has been whenever he comes over, I'll sleep like a baby. Holding my perfect boy is better than any sleep aid I've tried.

Ben is at my door shortly after six, looking like a dirty dream come to life like always. He's wearing exactly what I told him to, but it's even better in person. His tight, dark-wash jeans cling to his strong legs, making my mouth water. Desire stirs inside me to ask him to turn around and allow me to take in his bubble butt, but there's time for that later.

The black leather jacket I picked out from the back of his closet that he never wears gives him a bad-boy vibe that looks perfect on him, even though he's really a good boy at heart. Underneath the jacket is a navy blue T-shirt that clings to him, showing off his gorgeous muscles. To finish his outfit, I told him to wear his plain silver chain, which is the only jewelry he owns.

He's the sexiest man alive. I'd stare at him all night if we didn't have other plans.

My sweet boy is beaming, clearly not caring that I'm gawking a little. The look is almost enough to cause my heart to skip a beat. I mean, if that was physically possible and all.

"Damn, you clean up nice." I admire him, pulling him into my arms and planting a kiss on his lips, loving that he immediately melts into my embrace.

"I sure hope you think I look good. You were the one who picked out my clothes," he teases, and I chuckle.

"You have good taste in clothes. You just need a little help deciding what to wear. That's what daddies are for, after all." I wink at him, and his smile grows.

"Who knew how freeing it would be to let you choose my clothes each day? Our video calls where you pick my outfits have become one of my favorite things," he informs me, filling my heart with pride.

The fact that Ben loves something that also brings me immense joy is perfect. It confirms that I am doing a good job as his boyfriend and Daddy. It's something I wouldn't have thought possible three months ago, not with how busy my work life is. But here we are, thriving in our relationship.

"I'm glad you like it," I reply, turning to grab my car keys and a jacket for myself. "Did you eat?" I check with him as we walk to my car.

"Yup," Ben replies with a toothy grin. "I got your reminder text, so I grabbed a quick bite after practice."

"Such a good boy," I praise.

Ben's face lights up like it often does when I remind him how astonishing he is. But the thing is, I mean the words more than he could ever imagine. I'm not just saying them out of habit. I'm growing to love everything about him and want him to be fully aware of that.

"Are you going to tell me where we're going?" Ben asks, but I shake my head.

"It's a surprise. It wouldn't be a very good one if I told you what was about to happen."

Ben narrows his eyes in what I think is supposed to be a menacing glare, but the corners of his lips keep twitching, wanting to curl up, making it obvious that he isn't actually upset.

I've learned a lot of new things about Ben over the past few weeks, one being he *loves* Halloween and all things spooky. So, when I found out about a corn maze having fright nights all week long, I knew I had to bring him. It also doesn't hurt that it's only a thirty-minute drive from my house.

Ben's eyes land on a sign that appears like it's dripping in blood, telling us to *beware* when I pull up to the farm, and he starts to vibrate in his seat.

"Is this a scary corn maze?" Ben asks with pure excitement in his voice. His energy is contagious and brings a giant grin to my face.

"It is. Does that make you happy?"

"Happy doesn't even begin to cover how I'm feeling right now," he replies, leaning over to kiss my cheek.

My smile grows, which almost feels impossible, and I internally give myself a high-five for coming up with the perfect date night. I only wish I would have come up with the idea to plan something sooner.

Ben has been learning to trust me, but it's something that is going to take time to solidify. Taking him out more often will show him our relationship is real, and I'm not ashamed to be seen with him. I really should have done this the instant we made things official. I guess that's why they say hindsight is twenty-twenty.

"Sorry for not taking you out sooner," I tell him, but he waves me off.

"We've both been busy as f-fudge. When would we have been able to make a date work?" he replies, easing my worry and almost making me laugh at his near slip of a swear.

"You're right. Are you ready to be scared senseless?" I check, and he bobbles his head with a giant grin.

"Let's do this," he cheers, moving to open his door, but I stop him.

"Let me," I request, getting out and rushing to his side.

"I love how you treat me," he whispers, exiting the car, then wraps his arms around my torso for a tight squeeze.

"You deserve it, sweet boy. You have no idea how special you are to me."

We hold each other for a moment, then head to the ticket booth hand in hand. Once we're checked in and have our bracelets on, we wander around before hitting the corn maze, where people are stationed inside to jump out and scare the living daylights out of us.

"This is awesome," Ben states as we take in everything the farm has to offer.

There are booths set up with various activities like

pumpkin carving, apple bobbing, and face painting. When I first saw them, I thought they would be mainly for the younger crowd, but I've already passed my fair share of adults with their faces painted, which makes me smile. It's good to stay young at heart.

"Anything you want to try out?" I ask Ben who shrugs, continuing to look around.

It's when his feet stop shuffling and his brows shoot up that I'm aware he's found something that's caught his attention.

"They have a petting zoo," he whispers in an awe-filled tone, and I nod, trying to fight my smile. His excitement is adorable.

"Did you want to check it out?" I inquire.

"Yes!" he cheers, beelining it for the gated-off area.

I laugh, following along at a more leisurely pace. By the time I catch up to my excited boy, he's already hunkered down in the corner with a fluffy sheep on his lap.

"Can we get a sheep?" Ben asks with pleading eyes when I get over to him.

"I'm pretty sure there is a bylaw against keeping farm animals as pets in town," I reply.

Ben pouts but nods. "I guess that makes sense," he grumbles.

"Besides, we both already said we are too busy for a pet," I remind him.

He sighs. "But look how cute this guy is." The sheep *is* adorable, especially curled up on Ben's lap like he is. "And there's a goat over there in a Batman costume. Maybe I should give up my dreams of being a doctor and buy a farm."

"And how exactly would you pay for it?" I ask him.

Ben rolls his eyes and sticks his tongue out at me. "Ugh, why do you have to bring facts into my fantasy?" he complains.

I chuckle, shaking my head. "It's not a bad fantasy, but

how 'bout you volunteer on a farm first and figure out if you actually like it that much," I suggest. "Maybe after you've become a fantastic sports medicine doctor, you can buy a farm to hide away at after a long day."

Ben's eyes light up with joy like I just told him he could take the sheep home with him tonight. "That's a great plan. Would you like to live on the farm with me?"

Does Ben really see us still together then? I mean, I do, but I was also worried I was being crazy for thinking that already. But now that he's bringing it up, it's giving me hope that we'll make things last that long.

"I'd live on a farm with you," I tell him.

When he beams at my response, it fills my entire body with warm tingles.

We've only been dating for a month, but a future with Ben is something I want. Hopefully, my sweet boy feels the same way.

CHAPTER TWENTY-THREE

Ben

NO ONE HAS EVER TREATED me the way Ian does. It's like I'm the most special person in the world. It's addicting and something I would have been terrified of a month ago, but for some reason, I'm not running. Maybe it's because I'm really learning to trust this man.

Since we've made things official, he hasn't done one thing to give me even the slightest hint that he's going to leave anytime soon. In fact, he's done the opposite. He's shown me how crazy he is about me every single day. When we're together, he can't keep his hands to himself. It's like he's afraid I'm going to run, which I don't blame him for. And when we're apart, he's texting me, letting me know he's thinking about me or reminding me to do things I'd typically forget. The fact that he apologized for not taking me out on a date sooner, even though there literally hasn't been time for it, shows he actually cares.

I was stoked for our date tonight but had no idea what Ian had planned. I swear to God I almost had a heart attack when we pulled up to the farm, and I figured out where we were. Clearly, Ian has been paying attention when I talk because he planned the best date possible. Nothing would be able to top this. Haunted houses and fright nights are my jam. Honestly, anything scary is, but the corn maze is fucking perfect.

Ian's hand is in mine as we make our way through the

corn maze. My body is buzzing with the endorphins you get when you know something is about to scare the shit out of you. Some people hate getting scared, but I love it.

"You're shaking," Ian notes, and I beam at him.

"It's because I'm so excited."

He chuckles. "I've never met someone who likes to be scared as much as you do."

We're about halfway through the corn maze and have been scared a half dozen times or so already, but I'm still looking forward to it happening again. I don't care that I scream like a little girl every time it happens because that's part of the fun.

"Are you enjoying yourself?" I check, keeping my eyes peeled. It's been a hot minute since someone jumped out at us which means it's going to happen again soon.

"Personally, I wouldn't have come here by myself," he states. "But I'm having a great time watching you and how much joy this is giving you."

Fuck, Ian is obviously the best boyfriend ever. But how did someone like me get lucky enough to have him in my life?

We turn another corner, following the map on Ian's phone, but hit a dead end.

"Are we lost?" I ask with a smirk.

Ian glares at his phone. "I could have sworn we were here." He points to a section on the map that doesn't have a dead end.

"Well, clearly we're not," I reply, still smiling at him.

We backtrack a little and take a different turn, running into a man with a fake chainsaw. Well, at least I assume it's fake. I guess I really have no idea. I scream at the top of my lungs and let go of Ian's hand, running as fast as my legs will let me. Ian is behind me, but he's clearly having a hard time keeping up, and when I glance over my shoulder, I see the crazed man with a chainsaw is hot on his heels. I don't have the map, so I have no idea where I'm going, but I honestly don't care. I don't want to be caught by chainsaw man.

"You abandoned me," Ian says, panting heavily when he finally catches up.

"It's every man for himself when someone's trying to chop them into tiny little bits," I explain, making Ian laugh.

"Good to know for the future," he grumbles, but his smile is still in place.

"Aww… does my big stwong Daddy need me to pwotect him next time?" I ask in a baby-like voice.

He growls and pulls me into his arms. "You're such a brat sometimes," he tells me, smashing his lips to mine.

"I can't be good *all* the time," I reply once we break for air.

"And I wouldn't want you to. I love how full of life you are. Your bratty side is just a fun addition to who you are. But we both know, at your core, you're a good boy."

"We really need to find our way out of this maze because I'm ready for you to drill me so hard I'm going to have trouble walking," I inform Ian, who growls a little.

"How do you expect me to figure out a goddamn map when you put dirty images into my head like that?"

I lift my chin, smiling. "Consider it an incentive."

"Someone's wanting a spanking when we get home, isn't he?"

I nod quickly. "Yes, please."

"Then I guess we better find our way out," Ian responds, placing his hand on the small of my back and guiding me around another corner.

We hit a few more dead ends before finally finding our way out, heading directly to Ian's car once we do.

"Tonight has been the best night ever," I state while he drives us to his place.

"Best date of my life," he replies with a smooth grin, and I'd be lying if I said I didn't melt a little.

"And it's not even over yet. If I remember correctly, I was promised a spanking," I remind him.

Ian chuckles. "You've definitely earned one."

I wiggle in my seat from his words. Ian hasn't spanked me in some time, and I'm dying to have his handprints on my ass. I'll definitely feel it when I'm on the ice tomorrow, but I don't care. It will just be a reminder of who I belong to.

CHAPTER TWENTY-FOUR

AN EASY SMILE spreads across my lips as I saunter through the university halls. Ben and I have been together for six weeks now, and each day just gets better and better. He's everything I could have hoped for in a partner and a boy. And the doubts I harbored before we started our relationship about not being able to make things work have been completely wiped from my mind. Not only are we solid as a couple, but I also feel like I've become a better teacher.

"Professor Johnson," a female student calls out as I'm about to walk through my classroom's doors.

Pausing my footsteps, I turn to find Mindy Alistar approaching me with her brows pinched together.

"Good morning, Mindy. Can I help you?" I question and she nods, worrying her bottom lip between her teeth. "Why don't we have this discussion inside," I suggest, tilting my head toward the room.

She presses her lips together in a tight smile but walks into the classroom.

"I got the email you sent with my current grades, and I'm worried," Mindy states when we get to my desk. "I don't know why I'm not grasping the concepts, but I'm trying my hardest, and it feels like it's not good enough."

Tears pool in her eyes, and I sympathize with her. Her

hard work is evident in her grades, but obviously, she doesn't see that she *is* improving.

"Not every subject is easy for every student," I start, wanting her to know that just because this class is a challenge, it doesn't mean she's stupid. "When you first started this class, your grades were much lower than they are today. Your hard work is paying off, and you just need to keep it up. If you continue on the path you're currently on, you'll pass my class with no problems."

Her brows shoot up, and her eyes fill with hope. "Are you sure?"

I nod and offer her a warm, reassuring smile. "I'm positive. But if you feel like you need more help, I could get you the number for a tutor who works with some of my other students."

"I actually already hired one," she replies. "Maybe she's helping me more than I figured."

"Crazy immediate results are very rarely seen in situations like this, but your progress is evident."

Mindy's smile grows, and her posture straightens a little from my words. "Thank you, Professor Johnson. I appreciate you taking a moment to ease my worries."

"Any time," I assure her.

She leaves the classroom with more pep in her step, filling my heart with pride. This is why I got into teaching. I wanted to help kids learn and watch them grow, especially in subjects that challenged them.

With my classroom empty again, I move to set things up for the day, then check my phone to see if Ben has sent me a flirty morning text yet.

A groan pulls from my lips, and I shake my head, taking in the image of Ben's erection tenting his boxers.

Sweet boy: Morning wood is the worst.

> Me: I'm sorry you're suffering, but you better not touch yourself. I'll help take care of you after your game tonight.

> Sweet boy: You promise?

I laugh at his message while typing out my response.

> Me: I promise, but only if you're a good boy.

> Sweet boy: Silly professor, you should know by now I'm the BEST boy.

I smile at my screen because he isn't wrong. Ben is marvelous. He's everything I could have hoped for and nothing I ever thought I could have. Every day I spend with him I learn new things about him and myself. He might be younger than me by ten years, but we're growing together, and I love it.

TWO WEEKS LATER

My house is too empty and quiet as I lay on the couch, moping and watching Christmas movies.

It's Thanksgiving, and I really wanted to spend it with Ben, but he has an away game this weekend and is traveling.

I probably wouldn't feel this blue if it wasn't my first major holiday away from my family. We've always been the type to celebrate everything together, and I don't get to do that this year. If Ben were here, it would ease the ache a little, but unfortunately, that couldn't happen.

I'm barely paying attention to the movie when my phone

rings and a big smile spreads across my face when I see that Dad is calling.

"Hey, old man, how's it going?" I answer.

He laughs, and the sound envelops me like a warm hug. Man, I miss my family.

"I'm all right for a dinosaur," he replies, and I chuckle. "How are you doing?"

"Honestly?"

"Well, I didn't raise you to be a liar so an honest answer would be appreciated," he tells me like he's always done.

I sigh. "I miss you guys."

"You don't have anyone to spend the holiday with?" he inquires.

I haven't told my parents about Ben yet because two months isn't very long for a relationship. But I'm positive we aren't breaking up any time soon, so I guess now would be a good time to fill them in.

"I would have, but he's busy today, which is why I've been moping around and watching movies I've seen a hundred times," I explain.

"You're dating someone?" Dad asks, most likely double-checking he heard what I said correctly.

"I am," I reply, smiling so wide I bet it would be comical if someone saw it. "His name is Ben, and he's a hockey player. At least he will be until the end of the season. He's a student at GSU pursuing a career in sports medicine," I explain.

"A student?" he repeats. "Is that allowed?"

"Since he's not one of *my* students, it is. We just had to fill out some paperwork to inform the university of our relationship."

"Oh, that makes sense. So, he's quite a bit younger than you, I take it?" he questions.

"He's ten years younger, but neither of us is concerned with the age gap. He's a great guy, Dad. I know you'll love him when you meet him."

"Does that mean you're bringing him home for Christmas?" Dad asks.

"I haven't asked him yet. I was actually planning on doing something different this year," I fill him in. "Ben doesn't have parents, but he has an important person in his life, and from the sounds of it, he doesn't have the chance to see him often. I'm going to try to figure out a way to bring the two of them together over the holiday. I haven't spent a Christmas away from you guys, but Ben deserves something special. Is that okay with you?"

"Would it be okay with me if my son spends Christmas with the man he loves?" my dad asks, making my heart race. Ben and I haven't said the four-letter L word yet, but clearly Dad is picking up on how much Ben means to me simply by how I'm talking about him. "We'll miss you, but we have plenty more holidays to celebrate. You spend this one with Ben."

Dad's blessing makes me happy and eases some of the worry I was harboring around the hairbrained idea I've been conjuring up the last week.

"If something happens and the plan falls through, I'll let you know," I tell Dad.

"Sounds good," he replies. "Anyway, I should let you go. I just wanted to call and say that we love you, and we're here if you need us."

"Thanks, Dad. I love you too. Tell that to Pops, Mom, and MoMo, please."

"Will do, son," he assures me.

Once I'm off the call, I do a little digging on the internet, hoping I'll be able to find Coach Appleton in Los Angeles.

Surprisingly, it doesn't take long to find a guy that fits the profile of what Ben told me. I send him a message over social media, explaining who I am and what I'd like to do for Ben, then exit the app since I'm not expecting a reply right away. I turn my focus back to the movie that is now almost over and pray I found the right guy.

My eyelids are drooping, feeling like they weigh a million pounds as the movie plays, and I'm nearly asleep when my phone pings, alerting me that someone has sent a message on social media. I jolt awake and quickly reach for my phone, opening the app with fast fingers.

Calvin Appleton responded to my message, and my hands shake as I click on the icon to read the entire response.

> Calvin Appleton: Hi, Ian. Thank you for reaching out. I am Ben Cooper's childhood hockey coach. Your plan for Christmas sounds fantastic. I was actually planning on coming out to Michigan during that time anyway. Funny enough, I have a meeting at GSU for the opportunity to join their coaching team, and the only time that worked for everyone was during the Christmas break. I've been meaning to reach out to Ben, but I wanted to make sure the plans were solidified first. I would hate to get his hopes up and disappoint him. Anyway, if you're still interested in the three of us spending Christmas together, please let me know, and I'll be there.

My smile takes over my entire face, almost hurting as I type out my response immediately.

> Me: That's fantastic! And yes, the plan still stands, but I was kind of planning on keeping it a surprise. What do you think about that?

> Calvin Appleton: Sounds great. I'm looking forward to meeting you and spending some time with Ben. Fingers crossed, I land the job, and I'll be able to see him a lot more. That boy is like a son to me, and I'm so proud of the person he's turned out to be.

Me: I look forward to meeting you too. Ben is an amazing person, and he speaks highly of you. Thank you for being the one person from his childhood who didn't turn their back on him.

Calvin Appleton: No need to thank me. Ben deserved it.

I haven't met Calvin in person yet, but it's already obvious I'm going to like him a lot. With that piece of the puzzle solved, I develop more of a game plan to make this the best Christmas Ben has ever had.

CHAPTER TWENTY-FIVE

THE DOOR to my apartment shuts with a thud, and Bronny looks up from his textbook, smirking at me. "Oh, look who's home. I was beginning to think you moved out but didn't tell us," he jokes, and I stick my tongue out at him.

"Ha, ha, very funny," I reply dryly.

Bronny chuckles. "I'm just teasing you, man. How are things going with the professor?"

A lovesick smile spreads across my face, and I shrug, dropping my bag by the door and walking toward the living room. Ian and I have been dating for about two and a half months now, and honestly, things couldn't be going better. He treats me like I'm a treasure that needs to be protected at all costs. It's everything I ever could have hoped for in a relationship.

"Things are going amazing," I reply, noticing how dreamy my voice sounds. "Sorry I've been a little MIA."

Bronny waves me off. "Don't apologize. You're busy as fuck with hockey, and when you're free, you want to spend time with your man."

"That doesn't give me an excuse to bail on my friends. We should plan a games night sometime soon," I suggest.

"Sounds like fun. Just let me know when, and I'll try to make sure I'm free."

"Free for what?" Rio asks, exiting his room with wet hair.

"A games night," I tell him, and he grins.

"Oh, that sounds fun. We haven't had one of those in a while. Are you going to invite your hot professor boyfriend?"

"Would that be weird?" I ask Bronny since Ian is still technically his teacher, at least for a couple more weeks.

"I guess it depends when the games night is. I'd prefer it to be after the semester ends so he isn't my professor anymore."

"I could make that work. Maybe we could host it over Christmas break. We should also invite Monster and Sasha," I add.

"Sounds like a plan," Rio agrees. "Are you coming here after your game tonight or staying at Ian's?"

"Do you mind if I stay at Ian's?" I ask, feeling bad that I've been ditching my friends a lot over the past couple of weeks.

Rio waves me off. "Not at all, especially now that we have plans to hang out soon."

A big smile spreads across my face at how understanding my friends are. I'm glad they're in my life.

TWO WEEKS LATER.

TO SAY I'm happy the first semester is over would be an understatement. The past couple of weeks have been insanely busy for Ian and me, but we're finally over final exams and have a week off together. One I've been cherishing every minute of. In fact, I've been so lost in spending time together, I kind of forgot today is Christmas Eve.

Thankfully, I bought Ian's present over a month ago.

Ian, however, did not forget and wished me a Merry Christmas Eve first thing this morning. After breakfast, I figured out Ian had something up his sleeve. Unfortunately, he's refusing to give up information about the plan, like normal.

All I've been told is we're going on an adventure. The clothes he picked out for me are extra warm, which has me guessing that we're going somewhere cold. Since I love surprises, I've been a ball of excitement the entire time I dressed myself.

"I'm ready," I call out, exiting the bedroom and making my way to the living room where Ian is waiting.

"*Almost* ready," he corrects, then heads to the closet to pull out my winter coat, mitts, and beanie.

"Is the adventure outside?" I guess.

Ian nods. "Yes, but that's all I'm telling you, so stop trying to spoil the surprise."

I purse my lips at him, faking a glare. After three months of dating, Ian knows me very well and isn't shocked when my attitude makes an appearance. Although, I wouldn't really call it an attitude but more of a playful side.

"Come on, trouble. We have places we need to go," he states, and I hurry to put on my outside gear.

Once we're dressed all warm and cozy, we head to Ian's car, and he drives us downtown, which I'm kind of surprised about until my eyes land on the festivities.

"Are we going tobogganing?" I ask with wide eyes.

"Yup, plus there's hot cocoa and a snow angel competition," he informs me, and I squirm in my seat from the excitement bubbling inside my stomach.

"Best Christmas Eve ever!" I yell, making Ian laugh.

"We haven't even gotten to the best part yet," he tells me, and I stare at him like he's crazy.

How would it be possible to make today any better than it already is?

There is a knock on my window while I'm staring at Ian, trying to read his mind, which I'm failing horribly at. When I turn to see who it is, I suck in a deep, shaky breath, and my heart races.

"Coach Appleton?" I whisper with a shaky voice.

"Surprise, baby," Ian says quietly in my ear. "Now open the door and give the man a hug."

I do as I'm told, moving at the speed of a cheetah, almost hitting Coach with my door in the process.

"What are you doing here?" I ask, hugging him tightly.

"Your boyfriend invited me," he explains.

I wasn't aware it was possible to fall for Ian any more than I already have, but here we are. I'm shocked he did something so special like this for me. I haven't said the words yet, but I love him. Maybe I'll find the strength to say those words to him soon.

I let go of Coach Appleton and pull Ian into my arms.

"Thank you," I whisper into his ear.

"No need to thank me, baby. You told me how important Calvin was to you, and I wanted to make our first Christmas together extra special."

I wrinkle my nose at Coach's real name.

"I don't have to call you Calvin, do I?" I ask him. "It feels weird."

He laughs and shakes his head. "Coach works fine, just like I'll probably still call you Coop and not Ben."

I nod with a giant grin. "Ian is the only person here who calls me Ben."

"Did you want me to call you Coop?" Ian asks, but I wrinkle my nose again.

"No, it doesn't sound right coming from you."

Both Ian and Coach laugh as we head toward the festivities the town has put on.

Christmas hasn't always been my favorite holiday, but Ian might change that like he's changed a lot of things in my life. We've only been dating for three months, but I kind of don't see a future without him in it.

WE SPEND the majority of the day outside, enjoying all the festivities the town has to offer before heading back to Ian's place for some pizza. Apparently, tomorrow, he's going to make a full-blown Christmas meal for the three of us, and I can't wait.

I bet it's going to be the most delicious food ever, and I offered to help, but Ian insisted I should spend the time hanging out with Coach. Though, he's most likely just trying to save Christmas and to do that, it's best to keep me out of the kitchen.

After we're done with dinner, Coach heads back to his hotel, leaving me alone with the man who makes me happier than I've ever been.

"Thank you for everything," I whisper as we cuddle on the couch.

"You deserve it, baby," he assures me.

I move in his arms so we're face to face. "I love you," I tell him, staring into his gorgeous blue eyes. Before he repeats the words, I already know he feels the same way.

"I love you too," he replies, pressing his lips to mine.

"Best Christmas Eve ever," I whisper, earning me a chuckle.

"And the day isn't even over yet," he says, waggling his brows.

"Oooh, Christmas sex," I cheer, racing to the bedroom.

Ian's laughter echoes off the walls as he follows at a much slower pace.

Never in a million years did I think I would find a man like Ian.

I hope he stays in my life forever.

CHAPTER TWENTY-SIX

Ian

BEN HAD AN AWAY game over New Year's Eve, and instead of sitting at home alone, I took a quick trip home to see my family.

"You've been gone too long," Mom says, pulling me into her arms the second I open the door of Dad and Pops' house, squeezing me with the tightest grip that it almost hurts.

"At least let the boy take his coat off before you suffocate him to death," MoMo tells her, but Mom doesn't let go.

"He can take his coat off after I've got my hug in," Mom retorts. Once she's had her fill, she steps back and puts her hands on my shoulders. "You look good. Happier than when you left. I take it your boyfriend has something to do with that?"

I smile at her and nod. "He's the best thing that's ever happened to me."

Mom fakes a gasp. "What about us?"

"Beside my family, of course," I assure her.

"Okay, move out of the way. It's my turn," MoMo tells Mom who rolls her eyes but steps aside all the same.

"I can't wait to meet the guy who has you smiling like that," MoMo says, hugging me fiercely.

"I'm hoping soon, but unfortunately, he had a hockey game this weekend."

"Our turn," Dad says with Pops standing beside him.

I hug them, take off my coat, and head into the living room where Katy is.

"How come you didn't greet me at the door like the rest?" I ask.

"And give you a bigger complex? As if," she replies, standing to give me a big hug. "But I have missed you. I hate that you had to move for the job of your dreams and meet an amazing guy."

"I'm sorry," I reply, and she waves me off.

"No, you aren't," she counters.

I shrug. "I'm not. But it's not like I live *that* far away. We'll still be able to see each other."

She sighs. "You're right, but that won't stop it from being hard occasionally. I've spent the last twenty-eight years seeing you all the time. It's going to take some time to adjust to the change."

I nod because she isn't wrong. There's a strong possibility it would have been harder on me had I not started hooking up with Ben so early in the semester.

"Maybe I should come down there for a hockey game and see how talented your man is," she suggests, and I beam at her.

"I'd love that. I'll text you his schedule, and then you just let me know what day works for you. I still have that spare bedroom you're more than welcome to stay in."

"That sounds awesome. I'll make sure to bring earplugs. The last thing I need is to listen to you and your boyfriend boning," she jokes.

"Probably not a bad idea. Ben isn't a quiet guy."

She scrunches her nose and shivers. "Too much information," she grumbles.

The parents join us with a crap ton of food, which explains why they disappeared. We spend the evening laughing, catching up, and just spending time together. I wasn't aware of how much I missed my family until now. Hopefully, the next time I visit, I'll be able to bring Ben. I'm certain my entire family will love him, and I'm pretty sure he'll love them just as much.

IT'S BEEN a little less than two weeks since I saw Katy, and I'm beyond excited that she's coming to a hockey game. A bunch of Ben's friends are also sitting with us. I met Rio and Bronny a while ago since they're my boy's roommates, but Monster and Sasha are new to me. I'll admit, it's a little weird to be spending time with a guy who was my student last semester, but I'm sure the feeling will pass eventually.

"Holy shit, they're good," Katy says with a giant smile as the Koalas score a goal, and I nod.

"The first game I attended, the Koalas shut out the other team, and it was amazing," I tell her.

"It's because Ben is the best goalie ever," Rio states.

"He's fantastic," Katy agrees.

The puck flies across the ice in the grasp of the opposing team.

"Come on, Koalas!" Ben's friends shout as the opposing team approaches the Koala's net.

"You've got this, Ben," I say, even though it's impossible for him to hear my words of encouragement.

The other members of the Koalas are also in front of the net, trying to regain control of the puck but not succeeding for long. Both teams are fighting hard, but neither is gaining full control.

I'm not sure how long passes until it appears like one of our Koalas is about to make a break for it, but an opposing team member bulldozes into him, sending them both into the net with Ben, who falls, getting tangled up in the net.

Katy gasps and covers her mouth. "Holy shit."

"It's okay," Rio assures her. "Hard hits happen in hockey all the time. I bet everyone's going to be fine."

I've seen lots of hard hits since attending all the local hockey games, but none involving Ben, and it makes my stomach turn.

Other players of the Koalas start fighting with the members of the other team, probably pissed that their goalie was taken down like that. Even the two players who crashed into Ben are taking blows at each other now that they're up. People are screaming, and I'm not sure if I am the only one who notices Ben isn't getting up.

My heart is pounding the hardest it ever has. I can practically hear it.

Come on, Ben. Get up.

Eventually, the referees break up the fight, and people finally clue in that Ben is still lying in the net, barely moving. A medic comes out a moment later, and the arena quiets almost instantly as they assess him.

Everyone must sense that this isn't good.

"You said everyone was going to be okay," Katy yells at Rio as they help Ben off the ice on a stretcher.

I put my hand on my sister's shoulder to calm her down. "It's not his fault, Katy," I remind her, and she nods with a pout. I love that she hasn't even officially met Ben yet and is already protective over him. "I need to get down there and figure out what's happening. Can you catch a ride with Rio?" I ask her, then turn to Rio to confirm it's good with him as well.

"I've got her," he assures me. "You go be with your man."

I nod and rush out of the stands toward the area for players only. Of course, I'm stopped by a member of the Koalas team, but thankfully, they let me pass when I show them my GSU credentials.

"Ian," Calvin shouts, and I race over. Thank God he got

the job on the coaching team so I know at least one person in this area.

"Where is Ben? What the hell happened out there?" I ask once I'm close.

"He's being rushed to the hospital. When the players hit him, he twisted his knee and couldn't put any weight on it. They need to do X-rays and other tests to figure out how severe the injury is. Obviously, it's nothing life-threatening, but depending on how bad things are, he might not be able to play for the rest of the season."

I suck in a breath, and he nods. This has the potential to really mess with Ben's head. Hockey means everything to him, and if he has to sit out for the rest of the season, he'll hate every second of it. If the team loses their winning streak with him out, he's going to blame himself.

"Okay, I'm going to go be with him," I state.

"I'll be there once the game is over," he assures me, and I dip my chin, rushing out of the arena.

It almost feels surreal that this is happening right now, but I don't have time to panic. Ben isn't going to die, and my sweet boy needs me to be his strength right now. I can be that for him.

It's what daddies are for.

CHAPTER TWENTY-SEVEN

Ben

TEARS ARE STREAMING DOWN my face as the X-ray tech forces my leg straight so she can take a picture of my bones. I've never been a big crier, but I've also never experienced pain like this. I'm praying nothing is broken.

When the guys slammed into me, I instantly knew something was fucked from the way my leg tangled into the net, and I felt something pop.

What will I do if this injury prevents me from playing the rest of the season? I don't want to let my team down. Not after we've been doing so well all season. Our team has been working like a well-oiled machine, but all it takes is one piece not to work well, and everything falls apart.

Fuck!

Once the X-ray is done, I'm sent for an MRI for a different look at my leg. By the time I'm back in my room, I am spiraling and exhausted. But there is a man who always makes everything better, waiting for me when I arrive, and if I had the strength to leap into his arms, I would.

"You're here," I whisper, and he smiles as the nurse helps situate me in the hospital bed.

"I'll step out and give you two a moment," Melissa, the team's trainer, who has been by my side the entire time, states before leaving the room behind the nurse.

"Of course I'm here," Ian says, pulling up a chair and

sitting beside the bed. "I saw what happened and rushed over here once I found out where you were being taken. Sorry I wasn't here sooner."

I shake my head and reach for his hand, squeezing it tightly. "It's okay. You're here now, and that's all that matters. But where's your sister?" I ask, suddenly remembering I was supposed to meet her today.

"Rio said he would take her back to my place," he shares, and I nod, settling into the shitty hospital bed. "How are you feeling?"

"Like a truck ran over my leg," I grumble.

"I'm pretty sure that's to be expected. Have they given you any hints as to what's going on?"

I shake my head and sigh. "I wish, but so far, nothing. I've gotten an X-ray and an MRI. Now, I guess it's just a waiting game. Melissa has a solid poker face. If she's clued into anything, she isn't letting it slip."

"No matter what happens, I'll be here for you. You're going to get through this," he assures me, and I want to believe him, but I'm struggling.

Right now, all my thoughts are about letting my team down. If I had only been paying a tiny bit more attention, maybe I could have gotten out of the way before the other players slammed into me.

I'm not sure how much time passes when there is a knock on the door. I look up to see Melissa and Dr. Simmons, one of the school's sports medicine physicians, walking into the room.

"How are you feeling, Coop?" Dr. Simmons asks, standing beside my bed on the opposite side of Ian.

I tilt my head from side to side. "Been better, but the medicine the nurse gave me is helping with the pain."

"I'm glad to hear that," he says with a soft smile, but an emotion behind his eyes makes it obvious he's about to drop some bad news.

"How fucked am I?"

He presses his lips together, and I brace myself for the cold, hard truth. "You tore your ACL," he states, and I gasp.

I was praying it wouldn't be that, but I knew the possibility was there, especially when the pop radiated throughout my leg. ACL injuries are no joke. The recovery process is long, and I'm guaranteed to be out for the rest of the season. So much for bringing home another championship win.

"Thankfully, it's only a grade two injury, meaning the ACL is still in one piece, but it was stretched and partially torn. Surgery is going to be your best road to recovery. If you want to go that route, there is an orthopedic surgeon who will be able to operate Monday morning."

"What happens if I don't have the surgery?" I inquire.

"You won't ever be able to play hockey again, and there is a higher chance of reinjuring yourself in the future," he explains. "I highly recommend you choose to get the operation. It's a minimally invasive procedure and will give you the best chance of getting back to doing the things you love. I know you don't want to join the NHL, but would you never want to play hockey again, even just for fun."

He's right, of course. I've seen Dr. Simmons several times over my four years at GSU. He knows me and my love of the sport. If I don't have the surgery, I'll never get back on the ice which would be pure hell.

"Let's do the surgery," I murmur after a brief pause in the conversation.

"Good call," Dr. Simmons says with a nod. "Since your only injury is your ACL tear, we are going to discharge you. That will give you a couple of days to rest at home. The nurse will be back with paperwork soon and instructions for how to prepare for your surgery Monday morning."

"Thanks, Doc," I reply, feeling somewhat defeated.

He claps me on the shoulder. "I'm sorry this happened to you, but I promise this isn't the end. Yes, the recovery is going to seem like it lasts forever, but eventually, you'll be back to your normal self. Don't be too hard on yourself in the process."

With those parting words, he leaves, and I throw my head back against the bed, staring at the ceiling. It's easy for everyone to tell me not to beat myself up, but they aren't the ones who just had their world flipped upside down.

Ian squeezes my hand as I lay there silently. I love that he's here right now, but things are going to be different between us thanks to this injury which scares the shit out of me.

Thankfully, it doesn't take too long for the nurse to bring my discharge paperwork, along with the instructions for what to expect Monday, and Ian takes me to his place, where his sister and Coach Appleton are waiting.

When we knew I wouldn't be staying much longer at the hospital, we sent Coach a text to give him the new information and told him not to bother coming to the hospital. Of course, he still wanted to see me, so we agreed for him to meet us at Ian's place for a short visit.

"I'm Katy," a pretty brunette with piercing blue eyes, the same color as her brother's, says to me as I shuffle slowly into the house. "Can I help you get comfortable?"

Ian told me she's a physical therapist, so I trust her to know a thing or two.

"That would be wonderful. Sorry that we didn't get to meet on a better day. I promise my life isn't normally this chaotic."

She giggles and shakes her head. "I know you didn't plan to tear your ACL, so I'll let it slide this time," she teases. "But just because you're injured doesn't mean I'm going to go easy on you. I still plan to bulldoze my way into your life and make sure we're best friends before I leave."

I laugh as she guides me to the couch and places my leg on a few pillows to ensure it's elevated.

"I'd love that," I tell her, then turn toward Coach Apple-ton, standing and looking awkward with his hands in his pocket and his brows pulled together in a worried way.

"How are you feeling?" he asks once I'm situated.

I really wish people would stop asking that question. I mean, I understand why they're asking, but it's getting on my nerves. So, instead of answering, I raise a brow and shoot him a look that says *do I really have to reply?*

He shakes his head, blowing out a breath. "Sorry, I guess that's a stupid question. Coach Mason gave us all the rundown on your injury once the game ended. I'm sorry this happened to you, Coop."

I shrug my shoulder. "Shit happens."

"How long did they say recovery would be?" he asks. "Coach Mason only told us you would be out for the rest of the season."

"About six months. The paperwork says I'll be pretty sore and stiff for the first one to two weeks after surgery, but it will gradually get better," I explain. "It's gonna require a lot of physical therapy, but I guess one of the hardest parts is not overdoing it. If I push myself too hard, there is the possibility of making the recovery take longer."

"Your doctor isn't wrong," Katy supplies. "I've seen so many patients push it way too hard. You can end up doubling your recovery time if you aren't careful. The key to a speedy recovery is taking your time."

"That's going to be a challenge for you," Coach replies with a smirk.

I sigh. I've never been the most patient person, and I doubt this is going to be any different.

"I'll make sure he follows the doctor's orders," Ian assures Coach, and I have no doubt he's going to make sure I do absolutely everything I'm supposed to do.

While I've enjoyed Ian taking control over a lot of things,

I'm not sure how I am going to feel about him taking care of me while I'm injured.

Am I going to feel smothered? Is it going to be too much?

I have a strong suspicion Ian is going to want me to stay here after the surgery, but I'm going to want my space. Thankfully, my apartment has an elevator. I doubt I could fight Ian on staying at my place if there were only stairs.

"GSU has fantastic physical therapists, but if you ever have questions or want a second opinion, feel free to shoot a message my way," Katy offers, and I hand her my phone to put her information in.

"I'll probably do that when your brother is babying me," I tease.

"Oh, I doubt that my opinion will matter to him," she replies and sticks her tongue out at Ian when he grumbles. "He's always been the overprotective type. If he has something stuck in his head, even advice from a professional won't change his mind."

"I'm not that bad," Ian argues.

"Remember the time I sprained my ankle, and you wouldn't let me walk for almost two weeks even though the doctor said it would be fine?" she counters.

"The doctor wasn't around to witness how you winced every time you put weight on it," he grumbles.

"Which is normal and would have gone away the more I used it. Are you aware it's possible to actually hurt someone by resting too much?"

In response, he huffs out a breath through his nose, and Katy rolls her eyes. "Good luck with his stubborn ass," she whispers, and I chuckle. "Now, who's ready for some embarrassing stories about Ian?"

I laugh while Ian groans, and I already know that Katy is going to be someone I love having in my life.

We spend a good amount of time visiting, getting to know each other, and catching up, but eventually, it becomes hard to keep my eyes open. "I really hate to cut this visit short, but I'm exhausted. I think it's time for me to go to bed."

I'm pretty sure it's a mixture of the medication and the adrenaline wearing off that's causing me to be utterly exhausted. Besides, the doctor said I needed to rest, and that's what I'm going to do.

After Coach leaves, Ian helps me to his room and sits on the side of the bed once I'm comfortable. I didn't want to change since I was already in a pair of soft sweats and a light T-shirt. Dressing was a pain in the ass with a fucked-up knee.

"I'm going to send an email in requesting time off next week," Ian states, and I shoot him a *what the fuck* stare.

"Why the hell would you do that?" I ask.

He seems taken aback by my outburst, and his brows pinch together, clearly confused. "Because you're going to need someone to take care of you."

His Daddy instincts are in overdrive right now, but the last thing I want is for Ian to put his career at risk for me. "I'm going to be fine, and if I need help, I have roommates," I remind him. "Taking a week off work for no reason would be irresponsible, and I won't let you do it."

"You can't tell me what I can and can't do," he counters in a firm and demanding voice that lights an inferno deep inside me.

"But you can control *my* life?" I hiss out. "I know I've been letting you take the reins in many aspects, but you promised that we would talk through big things. You *telling* me what's going to happen isn't communication."

Ian's face falls, and he shakes his head, but I'm too pissed to care that he's upset. I grab my phone off the nightstand and call Rio, avoiding Ian's gaze while I do it.

"Hey, man, how are you doing?" Rio answers. "I wanted to check on you but figured you needed the rest."

"I appreciate that," I tell him. "I was actually hoping you could come pick me up from Ian's place."

Ian grabs my wrist, and I shoot him my meanest glare, which causes his brows to shoot up in surprise, and he lets go.

"Oh? I figured you'd want him to take care of you," Rio says, sounding shocked.

"I just want my own bed. Are you coming or not?"

"I'll come. Give me like ten minutes," he replies.

I thank him, then set the phone down and sit up, carefully moving to the edge of the bed.

"I'm sorry," Ian whispers. "But you don't have to go."

I shake my head. "It's best if we have a night apart. I'm tired and pissed off. I don't want to say anything stupid." My crutches are by the door, and I sigh because, of course, I need help when I just said I could do this on my own. "Can you grab my crutches?" I request quietly, though my jaw clenches, and thankfully, Ian doesn't argue.

"I'll get your bag," he states once I have my crutches, and I nod.

I'm not sure leaving really is the right move, but I wasn't lying when I said I was angry. I understand it's engraved deeply in him to want to take care of me, but I'm not a child, and he's not my actual father. He's my partner, and even though we have an unconventional agreement, it doesn't mean he gets to step in and take complete control of every aspect of my life. In fact, early on, he promised he wouldn't do that, and we would discuss anything major, like adults. I don't think I would be this upset if he had asked me what I thought about him taking some time off. The way he presented it as if it was already set in stone, hit a sore spot for me. One I wasn't even aware I had.

Slowly, I hobble to the front door, and Katy's brows shoot up when I walk past the living room where she's watching a show. "Where are you going?" she asks with a tilt of her head.

"Home. I want my own bed tonight," I lie.

She studies me for a moment but thankfully doesn't push the conversation.

"Can I stop by tomorrow before I head home?" she asks.

"That sounds nice," I reply with a small, tired smile.

Even though I just met Katy tonight, I already like her a lot. She's kind and caring, like her brother, but she's sweeter and softer than him. She's exactly who I would have wanted as a sister.

"I'll text you when I wake up," I assure her, and then make the rest of the journey to the front door.

Ian joins me with my bag, and I hate the awkward energy between us. I want to say something, but I have no idea what. Spending the night at my apartment will allow me some time to get my thoughts straight. Even though Ian doesn't want me to leave, it's best for us in the end.

Thankfully, it doesn't take Rio long to arrive, and Ian takes my bag out to the car as I carefully make my way there. "Would you mind calling me when you wake up?" Ian requests when I finally arrive at the passenger door. He seems unsure of himself, which is something I've never seen from him.

"I can do that," I assure him.

"I love you," he whispers and kisses me softly.

"I love you too," I reply, then fumble my way into the car.

I keep my eyes on Ian through the side mirror as we pull away. He doesn't move from his spot on the sidewalk until we're out of sight.

"So, what the fuck happened?" Rio asks once we've driven a couple of blocks.

"Ian pissed me off, and I needed a minute to breathe. I love him, but if he's going to smother me and put his career at risk, things aren't going to work out," I explain.

"Yeah, it's always better to take a small break instead of saying stupid things in the heat of the moment. But don't let things fester, either. You *do* eventually have to talk to him about how you're feeling."

I rub my forehead. "I know, but I need to sleep first. Hopefully, after a good night's sleep, I'll figure out why it triggered me the way it did because right now, I'm not even sure of the real reason."

"If you want to talk things out, I'm here for you," Rio offers.

"I appreciate it. Maybe I'll take you up on that in the morning."

When we arrive at our apartment, Rio brings my bag to my room and then leaves me to finally be alone for the first time in a long time.

The room is too fucking quiet as I lay still, trying to fall asleep. I miss Ian's breath in my ear and the weight of his body wrapped tightly around me. I haven't spent every night at Ian's, but I've spent enough to know I sleep better in his arms.

It was the right call to spend a night apart, but it doesn't mean I don't hate it. I just pray we're able to come up with a compromise tomorrow because if we can't, I'm going to have to spend a lot more nights on my own, and it's going to suck.

CHAPTER TWENTY-EIGHT

Ian

THE MORNING COMES FAR TOO QUICKLY, and my head aches from how horribly I slept. If I was lucky, I might have gotten three hours total, but none of it was restful. I tossed and turned all night. My thoughts drifted to how badly I messed things up, playing on repeat.

Even though it's only six in the morning, I get out of bed and make a pot of coffee since there is no chance I'll be able to sleep anymore, even if I wanted to.

Waiting for the coffee to brew, I keep thinking about what an idiot I was last night. I should have known telling Ben I was taking time off work instead of discussing it with him would trigger him. He likes it when I take control, but that was too big of a decision for me to make on my own. And it went against what I promised him when we first started our relationship. It probably reminded him of all the times people forced things on him when he grew up in the foster system. He wasn't able to make a decision on anything big, and here I am, doing the same thing. Letting me take over the tedious things that Ben doesn't like was easy, but this was a step too far, especially with no communication.

I just wanted to take care of him, and the nurse said the first week after surgery would be a challenge. I guess I just went into autopilot and figured the obvious choice would be to take time off work. Clearly, that was the wrong decision, but how do I fix it?

"How are you?" Katy asks while I'm staring into the coffee pot, and I jump a little. "Sorry, I didn't mean to scare you."

I wave her off. "It's fine. I was just lost in thought and didn't hear you. What are you doing up this early anyway?"

"I've stopped being able to sleep in," she mumbles. "It's a curse, but thankfully, coffee cures it. Mind pouring me a cup?"

It's then I see the coffee is finished brewing. I was more caught up in my head than I figured.

I pour us both a cup, then join my sister at the kitchen table.

"Did you and Ben get into a fight last night?" she asks once we've both taken a couple of sips.

"Not really a fight, but I put my foot in my mouth, and Ben wanted the night to cool off," I explain.

"I figured something like that happened. Ben looked angry and confused when he walked by the living room until he noticed I was still there. He quickly concealed his real emotions, but it was obvious he didn't really miss his own bed."

I nod but don't reply. What else is there to say? Katy doesn't have magic to fix this mistake. It's up to me to figure this out on my own.

"Did you want to watch some TV or just be left alone to wallow in your mistakes?" Katy asks.

I chuckle and shrug. "TV sounds good," I respond.

We refill our mugs before heading to the living room to watch some stupid comedy rerun that takes my mind off Ben, at least for a little while.

I fell asleep on the couch halfway through the second episode, and I have no idea what time it is when my phone buzzes in my pocket, waking me. I sit up and swipe the screen open, smiling when Ben's name appears, but the small amount of happiness I had is quickly wiped away as I read the message.

> Sweet Boy: I invited Katy over to hang out before she leaves, would you mind not coming with her? I want to talk, but we need to do that later and by ourselves.

"Did Ben text you?" Katy asks from the living room with her suitcase by her feet. She's dressed now and is nibbling on her lower lip, something she's done since she was a child when she's nervous.

"He did."

"Are you okay if I go over there by myself?" she asks, then quickly adds, "I won't go if you don't want me to."

I shake my head. "No, you should go. I like that the two of you hit it off. I understand why he doesn't want me there right now. I don't like it, but I get it."

"I promise I'll come back and visit again soon," Katy says, then joins me on the couch to give me a big hug.

"I can always try to come out there and visit you too," I reply.

"Our parents would love that," she tells me. "Maybe I should move away, too, because they are way too involved in my life right now with me the only child close to them."

I chuckle. "Maybe GSU will be hiring a new physical therapist one day."

Katy's eyes light up. "That would be awesome. Then I could bug you all the time like I used to when we were younger."

I fake a shiver, trying to fight a smile. "That sounds like a nightmare."

She gives my shoulder a gentle shove, then stands up. "Love you, big brother. I'll see you soon."

"Love you too, brat. I promise I won't be a stranger."

After she leaves, I spend a good amount of time staring at the ceiling until I decide that I'm being an idiot, and there are better things for me to do with my time, like grading papers. So that's what I do.

Staying stuck in my head isn't going to help things with Ben. The only thing there is to do is wait and stay busy doing it.

CHAPTER TWENTY-NINE

WHEN KATY SHOWS up at my apartment, I'm a little nervous she's going to be mad that I asked her to leave her brother behind, but thankfully she isn't.

"How pissed is he?" I ask when she sits on the couch.

I have myself situated in a recliner with my foot on a few pillows to keep it elevated, according to the instructions I received from the nurse.

"Not pissed, more like kicking himself for being an idiot," she states.

I sigh, then give my head a shake. "Okay, no more talk of your brother. This is our time, and I refuse to spend it being upset," I tell her.

She giggles. "Sounds like a plan. What did you want to do?"

"Do you like *Mario Party*?" I question, and her face lights up, which is the only answer I need. "The controllers are under the TV." She quickly moves to grab them so we can start a game.

"Are you playing *Mario Party* without me?" Rio asks as we're getting things set up.

"It's not too late to join us."

That's all I needed to offer because he grabs a controller and plops down beside Katy.

"Should we invite Bronny too? Don't need him being all mopey because we forgot about him."

Rio shakes his head. "He has a wrestling match this afternoon. He's already at the campus getting ready with his team."

"Oh, right, I completely forgot about that." I normally like to support my friends and watch their sports, but Bronny has a weird superstition about his friends being at his events, so we never attend out of respect for him. But his one coach always takes high-quality footage, and Bronny shows us after each match.

"Perfect, let's get this party started then," I announce, hitting the button to start the game.

We spend the next hour battling in mini-games and talking smack every chance we get. Katy shows us she has a mouth I wasn't expecting from such a pretty woman. She's the queen of talking shit, and it makes me like her even more.

By the time Katy has to leave, my stomach hurts from laughing ridiculously hard, and I feel a lot lighter than I was before she came over.

"Did you want me to drive you to my brother's house on my way out of town?" she asks, causing my stomach to knot with anxiety.

I should take her up on the offer, but I find myself shaking my head instead. "I'm sorry. I still need a little bit more time," I murmur.

"I get it, but don't take *too* long. Just like in physical therapy, sometimes you have to work through the pain to get the results you want," she reminds me before leaving.

Rio leaves not long after Katy to go hang out with Sasha, telling me to call him whenever I need a ride. I wanted to be alone, but now the apartment is too quiet. So, I shoot a text off to Coach, asking him to come over for a visit.

"I'm surprised you aren't at Ian's," he says when I open the door for him, which is awkward on crutches.

"We kind of got into an argument after you left last night," I explain, slowly returning to my chair.

"What about?" he asks, making himself comfortable on the couch.

"Ian told me he was going to take a week off work to look after me," I tell him, and when I say the words out loud, it sounds stupid that it made me so angry.

"And it made you feel like you didn't have a say, didn't it?" he guesses, and it still boggles my brain at times that he knows me as well as he does. I'm happy he's working at GSU now, and we can have chats like this in person.

"That's exactly how I felt. Maybe I shouldn't have gotten that upset, but it was like his words hit a detonation button, and it completely fired me up."

"It actually makes complete sense that you lost your cool," Coach responds. "You never had a say in any big decisions made in your life when you were growing up. You were just told what was going to happen, whether you liked it or not. You had no control over anything, and when Ian told you his plan, you felt like that little child with no choice again. But you aren't a child, and you do have a choice. You snapped because you didn't want to feel powerless again." My eyes go wide as he nails it on the head. "But Ian most likely wasn't thinking about that when he was talking to you last night. He was thinking about the man he loves who was injured and needs someone to care for him. Yes, he should have gone about it differently, but the underlying meaning was good. He didn't want to take away your power... he just wanted to help you."

My heart hurts as I nod. "You're right," I whisper. "And now I feel like even more of a fool."

"Don't. You reacted to a trigger from a trauma that runs a lot deeper than you knew. Don't fault yourself for that. Now you just have to explain that to Ian and discuss what you're going to do as a team."

"Ian wants to take care of me. It's a huge part of who he is, but I'm worried that by taking time off work, he'll put his career in jeopardy," I voice. "He's worked extremely hard to get to where he is, and I won't let him put that on the line. I'm afraid that he's blinded by love right now, and one day, he isn't going to feel the same way, and if this does affect his job, he'll resent me for it."

"Not everyone is going to leave you," Coach says. "I'm still here, and it's not because I'm some sort of unicorn. The people who raised you in the foster system were idiots for not seeing how amazing you are. They were foolish for not wanting to keep you. If they had spent the time to get to know you, they wouldn't have let you go. The people in your life now are aware of the treasure of a person you are and are willing to put in the hard work to keep you."

Emotion bubbles in my throat, and I blink back tears. I wasn't expecting Coach to become all sentimental like this, but his words are like a balm to my broken heart.

"Would you mind driving me to Ian's?" I ask when the frog in my throat has disappeared, and my voice is no longer raspy from all the emotions.

"That I can do, son," he says, and a tear breaks loose at his words.

I always wanted a dad growing up, but now that I think about it, I kind of had one. Even though it was never on paper, Coach Appleton was my father, and I'm so fucking lucky I have him in my life. Maybe one day I'll ask him if I can call him Dad because Coach is starting not to feel right anymore.

CHAPTER THIRTY

IT'S late in the afternoon when there is a knock at my door. I wasn't expecting anyone, and Ben hasn't reached out, so I have no idea who it could possibly be. It's probably just a door-to-door salesman, but I make my way to open it, none-theless.

I almost gasp when my eyes land on my sweet boy.

"Surprise," he says with a small smile. "Mind if I come in?"

I step to the side and wave him in. "Of course, sorry, I just wasn't expecting you."

"I guess I should have told you I was on my way, but it was kind of a spur-of-the-moment decision," he explains, slowly making his way to the living room. "I was talking with Coach, and he helped me figure out a lot of things."

"I'm glad. Did you want to talk to me about them?" I ask as we enter my living room.

I pull the coffee table closer to the couch and put a pillow on it for Ben to rest his leg on. He smiles as he takes a seat, and I sit beside him.

"Yeah, but first I want to say I'm sorry for bolting last night. When you told me you were taking a week off work, it was like there was no room for discussion, and it triggered me. All my life, I had no control over big decisions, and I was afraid that was happening again. I love you and like it when you help me make decisions, but I also refuse to give up all of my power to you. If you need a partner who's willing to do that, it's not me."

I shake my head, taking his hand in mine. "I don't need that. I didn't clue in until after you got upset that I sounded like such a dictator. I should have figured out sooner that would trigger you, but I was too caught up in my desire to take care of you."

He squeezes my hand and offers me a small smile. "Coach pointed out that might be the case. My fear of being abandoned also played a part in my reaction last night," he informs me. "I was afraid that by taking a week off work, you could possibly be jeopardizing your job, and if something happened, you'd end up resenting me over it once your love for me started to fade."

"Baby, my love for you will never fade. I'm not going anywhere. No matter what," I assure him.

"Coach was able to get me to see that too. He also made me realize that he's the father I always wanted. I want to ask him if I can call him Dad."

"I think he'd like that," I agree, wrapping my arms around him.

My sweet boy has gone through so much in his life, and I hate that my actions brought up such negative emotions for him last night. But I'm glad he was able to have a heart-to-heart with Calvin and finally know how loved he really is, not just by me but by his chosen family.

"I promise I'll talk to you about any big decisions going forward and never make them without your input again," I whisper into his hair.

He mumbles his thank you into my chest. I'm sure our position isn't the most comfortable for him, but I also don't want to let him go just yet. I was terrified last night that he might let this be our breaking point and try to push me away, but I'm thankful it didn't and that he had someone like Calvin to talk things over with.

Ben's stomach grumbles after a little while, and I pull back to stare into his eyes. "When did you eat last?"

A guilty expression crosses his face, and he bites his lower lip. "Um… do I have to answer that question?"

Under normal circumstances, I'd give him trouble for not eating, but I'm going to let it pass this time because he's been through a lot in the last twenty-four hours. "You don't have to answer it, but I am going to make you something to eat," I tell him, making my way to the kitchen.

Ben chuckles behind me, and seconds later, the hum of the television fills the space, bringing a smile to my face. I'm beyond happy to have my boy back in my house and for the stomach-turning anxiety to be gone. I'd still like to take next week off work, but I'll let Ben make that decision because it's not worth losing him over. I'll still find a way to take care of him whether I can be with him twenty-four seven or not.

Since I don't want to spend too much time away from Ben, I make a quick sandwich and then cut up some fruit and vegetables to go on the side. With the plate in hand, I head back to the living room and place it on Ben's lap.

"Eat up, sweet boy," I instruct. "It's even more important to take good care of yourself right now. Your body needs all the strength it can get to heal."

He beams at me and takes a bite of his carrot. "Yes, Daddy."

The word sends shivers of desire throughout my body, and I lean in to give him a kiss and nip at his lips. "Damn, I wish I could have you," I whisper against his lips.

"You could, but we just have to be creative," he replies, causing my cock to perk up even more at the idea.

I groan and shake my head. "There isn't any way that would put my mind at ease enough. I couldn't live with myself if I hurt you more than you already are. We'll just have to be patient." Ben pouts, and I give him another quick peck before sitting back. "Besides, you still have to eat."

Ben huffs out an annoyed breath through his nose but begins to eat, and I settle in to watch the show with him.

"Would you be okay if I made a call to see if I can take Monday off?" I ask him once he's finished his food. "I'm aware you don't want me to take the entire week off, but I would like to be there for you on the day of your surgery."

Ben silently contemplates my offer, and my heart races a little with worry. Is he going to say no? When he eventually nods, I almost let out a sigh of relief.

"I'd be okay with that. Would you mind if I stayed at my apartment while I recover?" he requests. "Obviously, you want to take care of me, but with your work schedule, having my roommates around might make more sense. You can come over whenever you want and even spend the night if you'd like."

I love that he feels empowered enough to ask the question, so, of course, I agree. "I could make that work. And you're right. If I'm working, having your friends around in case you need help would be best. But also know that if there's an emergency, I want you to call me."

"I promise I will," he replies with a smile.

We should have had this conversation yesterday if I wasn't such an idiot, but I'm glad we're having it now. This is how relationships are supposed to be. Give and take and open communication at all times.

CHAPTER THIRTY-ONE

IT'S the morning of my surgery, and I'm a nervous wreck, waiting for my name to be called. Thankfully, Ian is by my side, holding my hand and giving me all the strength possible.

I'm glad he took the day off to be here today. I still stand by my decision not to let him take the rest of the week off, but I'm sure I would be a lot more scared if I were here by myself right now. Obviously, Calvin would have come if I asked, but I'm glad it's Ian who is here.

I've been trying to stop referring to Calvin as Coach in my head, but it's still a little weird. I haven't had time to have the conversation about calling him Dad yet, but I'm hoping to have it sometime this week. I'll have a lot of spare time on my hands while I recover, and I'm hoping my friends and found family will visit often.

The school has agreed to give me two weeks off classes, and I'll take advantage of them. After the two weeks are up, it will be all schoolwork and physical therapy. I'm going to despise the downtime, but it will also be nice to have a mental health break. I need the time to deal with the fact I won't be playing college hockey anymore, and the next time I set foot on the ice, it will be as a regular man, not a player.

"Benjamin Cooper?" a woman calls out.

I'm shaking as I raise my hand, and she walks over, grabbing the wheelchair handles.

"You've got this," Ian reminds me with a warm smile and one more squeeze of my hand. "I'll be here waiting when you're done."

I nod and take a deep breath, telling the lady I'm ready to go, and she wheels me toward the Pre-Op area.

AS PROMISED, Ian is waiting when the surgery is over. Even though I'm so ridiculously uncomfortable, it's not even funny, I can't help but grin when my eyes land on him.

"Time to bring you home, sweet boy," he tells me in a quiet voice, and I nod as he helps me to his car.

The drive to my apartment isn't very long, but I'm beyond excited to get out of the car when we arrive. Being cramped in a vehicle isn't the most pleasant feeling following an ACL repair surgery.

It takes a lot longer to get up to my apartment than it used to a week ago, but with Ian's help, I eventually arrive, and even though I shouldn't be, I'm surprised to find Calvin sitting next to Rio on the couch.

"How did the surgery go?" Calvin asks, and I shrug.

"I was asleep for most of it, and now I'm achy all over, but I guess it could be worse," I respond, and he chuckles.

"I hate to say hi and bye, but I have to get to my classes," Rio says, standing to grab his backpack. "If you need anything from the store, I'm stopping there after school, so send me a text."

I nod and hobble over to the recliner once he's gone.

"How 'bout I go pick us up some food," Ian offers.

Calvin might not understand what's going on, but I know

Ian is giving us some time alone to have the conversation I've wanted to have.

"Sounds good," I reply, and he quickly kisses me before heading out.

As I move to make myself comfortable, I wince a couple of times, and Calvin's face pales. "Are you sure you're okay?" he questions. "Do you need me to get you anything?"

I let out a little laugh and wave him off. "I'm going to be sore for a while. I just have to get used to it, but there is something I wanted to talk to you about."

"Is that why Ian left so quickly?" he asks.

"Probably, but it's not like we discussed it beforehand since we didn't know you were going to be here."

"I just wanted to make sure you were okay. I didn't realize how badly I would be rattled with you having a surgery like that," he confesses.

"It's because we're family, and families care when the people they love are hurt," I reply.

"Yeah, that's it. So, what did you want to talk about?" He tilts his head and studies me for a minute, kind of like he's trying to read my mind and find the answers before I speak them.

"I wanted to talk about us being a family," I start. "Growing up, you were truly a father figure to me, and after talking the other day, I figured out that just because you weren't my father on paper doesn't mean you aren't still my dad in all other aspects of the word. I've always called you Coach, but that name doesn't fit us anymore, and Calvin isn't right either. So, I was wondering if I could call you Dad?"

Calvin's brows shoot up, and he appears dazed for a moment before a soft smile spreads across his face.

"I'd like that. You've always felt like a son to me," he whispers, and a rush of warmth and love fills my chest. "If I could have adopted you when you were younger, I would have, but I just didn't have the means to raise a child."

I shake my head. "You did more for me than you'll ever know. I don't care that you didn't adopt me. At least you stayed. You loved me and did the best you could, and that's a lot more than the people I was actually living with. You're my dad no matter what blood or birth certificates say, and nothing will ever change that."

Dad stands once I've finished my last sentence and gives me an awkward hug because of the way I'm sitting, but I cling to him, nonetheless.

"I'm never leaving you," he whispers in my ear, and I have to fight back tears. That appears to be a new habit for me. Hopefully, I'll go back to normal when I'm off the meds and healed.

Words like the ones he said would normally have made me scoff because everyone used to leave me, but this time, I believe them. Calvin is my dad, and he isn't going anywhere because that's what people who really love you do.

They stay.

This is how I know Ian will be in my life for the long haul because he loves me with his entire heart. Growing up, I had no idea what love was, but now I do, and I'm glad I found it in Ian and my dad. They are two different types of love, but both very important, and I'm done running from it. I am going to embrace this newfound happiness and love and never let either of them go. They are my family, and I'm lucky to have them in my life.

CHAPTER
THIRTY-TWO

Ian

EIGHT MONTHS LATER

SOMETIMES, I'm pretty sure Ben is a crazy person, but I still love and support him just the same. That's why I'm sitting at a little rink at nine in the morning on a Saturday in the middle of September, cheering on a bunch of kids as they stumble across the ice.

After Ben recovered from his surgery, he came across a posting for a volunteer kid's hockey coach at a local rink and immediately signed up. Even though he's still a student and now in med school, he wanted to take on the responsibility of helping these kids out. Kind of like Calvin did for him. So, most of his free time is spent at the rink coaching these kids to be the best hockey players they can be. He's never been happier.

When Ben first mentioned the coaching gig, I thought he was crazy, and honestly still do, but I understand now why he wanted to do it. Some of the kids on the team are terrible, but they always leave the arena with giant smiles, and I'm not sure that would be the case if they had a different coach. Ben doesn't care how well they play, just that they try their hardest and never give up. These kids might not grow up to be NHL players, but by having a fun and supportive coach like Ben, they might develop a strong work ethic and a love for themselves. At least that's the goal.

Once the game is over, I make my way to the locker room and smile, overhearing Ben praising the kids. That's how he ends any game, whether they win or lose. Maybe that's why the kids are always smiling.

"I'll see you all on Wednesday," Ben promises the kids at the end of his speech, offers them all a high-five, and then leaves them to change.

"You're good with them," I say once he's joined me in the hallway.

"It's easy because they're all awesome," he replies with a big grin. "Tommy is going to lock up, so we're free to head out now."

Tommy is the owner of the rink and used to coach the team before Ben came along. He's a really great guy but wanted a little more downtime. Although he's here just as much as Ben, so I'm not sure how much downtime he's really getting.

"Perfect, that means we'll have time to change before we need to be at the restaurant," I say.

"You made reservations?" he asks, and I nod.

"It's a special day," I explain but clearly Ben doesn't remember what date it is, which is fine by me. He's never been good at remembering any occasion. In fact, he would have forgotten his birthday if I didn't remind him.

"Why is it special?" he inquires as we walk to the car.

"We've been together officially one year today," I tell him with a big grin. "Happy anniversary."

Ben's brows shoot up, and a look of sheer panic crosses his face. "Shit. I mean shoot. I completely forgot, and I didn't get you anything."

I chuckle and squeeze his hand. "It's okay. I knew you wouldn't remember. That's why I already have the perfect gift for the both of us waiting at home."

His face quickly changes from terror to intrigue, but if he thinks I'm going to ruin the surprise, he doesn't know me at all.

"We better hurry so we can start celebrating," Ben says, tugging my hand, and I can't help but laugh. I hope he's always going to be this eager.

I let my sweet boy drag me to the car and then drive us to our house. It took a lot of convincing, but Ben agreed to move in over the summer after a friend of his needed to find a new place to stay. He didn't want his roommates to have to find someone to take over his room, but when his friend found himself in the lurch, it was a match made in heaven. Ben was free to move in with me, and Rio and Bronny didn't need to look for a new roommate.

"So, where's the present?" Ben asks the second we walk through the front door, and I shake my head at him with a giant grin.

"Go have a shower, and I'll retrieve it," I tell him and chuckle as he races down the hall.

He doesn't have a clue what I have planned, but he clearly doesn't want to risk missing out on anything, either.

While Ben showers, I pull out a box from under our bed where I stored his present. We've experimented with toys over the last year and talked about Ben wearing a plug when we go out but haven't actually done it yet. I figured tonight would be the perfect time. I'll stretch him and plug him before we go out for dinner, when we come back, I'll be able to directly sink into him and fuck him silly.

It doesn't take my sweet boy long to clean himself and join me in the bedroom in all his naked gloriousness. I'll never get over how drop-dead gorgeous he is. I could spend every second of every day worshiping his body for the rest of my life and be the happiest man on earth. Unfortunately, that doesn't pay the bills, so I have to take breaks to work.

"Get on the bed on all fours," I instruct once I've gotten

my fill of him.

Ben eagerly obeys and positions himself by my side. "Are you going to tell me what the present is now?" he asks with a lusty grin.

I hold up the new butt plug I bought for him that is a lot larger than anything we've played with. His mouth drops open for a second, then he licks his lips and wiggles his ass, clearly wanting it inside him immediately.

"I'm going to plug this perfect hole," I tell him, tapping his entrance with my index finger. "Then we're going to go out for dinner. When we get back, I'm going to fuck you so hard you'll have trouble walking tomorrow. And once I've filled your channel with my cum, I'm going to put the plug back in, sealing my load inside you until I decide to let it out."

Ben's entire body shivers with anticipation, and he pants with need. "That sounds perfect, Daddy," he whispers. "Please put it in."

I chuckle and squirt a decent amount of lube over his hole and begin to stretch him with my fingers. I normally enjoy taking my time with this process, but I want to hurry tonight so I'm able to enjoy the view of the plug stretching him wide.

"You look impeccable," I tell him once the plug is in place, and the soft, sexy smile that Ben offers me is like a reward in itself.

"I feel perfect," he replies quietly and shakes his ass a little.

I give it a gentle smack that has him squealing and probably clenching around the plug before standing. "Time to get dressed. You know I hate being late."

Ben pouts but takes my hand when I offer it to him. I already have his clothes picked out and help him get dressed, loving the way he allows me to do this for him.

Ben really is the perfect boy, and I can't put into words how happy I am that I found him. As I vowed silently to myself almost a year ago, I'm never going to let him go.

CHAPTER THIRTY-THREE

Ben

DINNER IS A DELICIOUS TORTURE. The food is divine, but I'm very well aware I have a giant plug in my ass the entire time. It doesn't help that Ian's hands have been on my body every second he can. They are innocent touches to the average person, but they have me aching for more.

By the time dessert rolls around, I'm dying to get home and have Ian fuck me into the mattress. To have him own my body and leave me feeling how well he uses me for days.

"Do you not like your cheesecake?" Ian asks with a smirk.

"It's fine," I grumble, but don't take another bite.

"Is something wrong," he inquires with a tilt of his head.

This time, I glare at him. "You know exactly what's wrong."

"I do?" he asks in fake shock, and I roll my eyes.

"You keep touching me, teasing me, and staring at me with those gorgeous blue fuck-me eyes and all the while, I have a giant butt plug in my ass," I hiss out at him in a hushed voice. "I'm so hard I'm afraid my penis is going to fall off. All I want is to be home already so you can finally make good on your promise, but you're enjoying being a masochist tonight and taking your sweet time, even though you're well aware that it's killing me."

Ian chuckles. "All you have to do is ask nicely, my sweet boy, and I'll pay the bill and take you home."

"Please, Daddy. I need you so bad," I beg shamelessly.

Ian flags down the waiter and pays our bill as soon as he has it. Ian isn't a liar, but I wasn't expecting him to actually pay so quickly, not that I'm complaining. I need us to get home before I come in my pants.

Ian drives us home, never exceeding the speed limit, though I wish he would. The second we pull into the driveway, I bolt into our house and head directly to the bedroom.

"Someone sure is a needy boy," Ian says once he arrives behind me.

"Needy doesn't even begin to describe how I'm feeling right now," I complain.

"Get naked then," he commands.

He doesn't even have the last word out before I'm stripping out of my clothes, which makes him laugh. Ian takes his time getting undressed like he doesn't see my cock leaking an insane amount of precum. Like he isn't aware of how fucking desperate I am right now.

"Get on all fours near the edge of the bed," he instructs once he's naked.

I obey his command at lightning speed and shiver when he runs his hand down my spine. "You're such a good boy," he whispers. "So fucking perfect for me."

"I need you, Daddy," I whimper. "*Please* fuck me."

Ian doesn't respond, and for a second, I'm afraid he's going to scold me for swearing, but how exactly does he expect me to keep a clean mouth when I'm this horny? Thankfully, my worries are pushed away when the audible click of the lube bottle sounds out, letting me know that he's getting himself ready. Seconds later, there's a tug on the butt plug as he gently removes it, leaving me empty. Thankfully, though, that emptiness only lasts for a short time.

Ian slams into me with one thrust, and I cry out as he fills me with his perfect cock.

"You like that, don't you?" Ian asks.

I nod but struggle to find the words to respond with.

"You love it when Daddy fucks you hard," he states, doing exactly that.

His hips move fast and hard, giving me everything I've been dreaming of all night. My needy mewls, Ian's growls, and the sound of skin slapping together fill the room as he fucks me exactly how I love it.

We've barely started when the telltale signal of my orgasm approaches, and I gasp.

"Daddy, I'm close," I warn him.

"Come when you need to," he tells me, and I sigh in relief.

Ian doesn't slow his punishing pace, and by the way his grunts get louder, I'm sure he won't be far behind.

Surprisingly, I don't come as fast as I figured I was going to. Even though his cock is pushing me to the edge, it's like it's not enough. Eventually, Ian reaches around my body and grabs my cock, stroking it in time with his thrusts, finally giving me that little bit extra I needed.

"Fuck!" I cry out, reaching my climax and shooting my jizz all over Ian's fist and the bedspread.

"Jesus," Ian chokes out when my channel clamps down around him, and his movements become jerky.

It only takes a few more thrusts, and he's joining me in the bliss of an orgasm. Did he come so hard that he saw stars like I did?

As promised, Ian slides out of me and replaces his cock with the butt plug once again, trapping his cum deep inside my channel. Once it's in place, he rips the top blanket off the bed and tosses it to the floor before grabbing my waist and pulling me into his arms.

"I love you so fucking much," he whispers, and I smile against his neck.

"Not as much as I love you," I reply.

I thought I wouldn't find someone to love me like Ian does. He's everything I ever wished for and more. Some days,

I still don't believe I deserve his love, but I also refuse to let him go. He's mine now, forever, and always.

The End

Thank you so much for reading Testing the Goalie! If you loved this story please <u>leave an honest review!</u>

Up next we have Sasha and Rio in - Teasing the Winger: *an m/m annoyances to lovers college soccer romance.*

What happens when you start to develop feelings for the guy who has annoyed you since the moment you met him?

Coming to Amazon and Kindle Unlimited July 11th. <u>Pre-Order Today.</u>

ALSO BY LAURA JOHN

*** Indicates M/M romance

GSU - M/M COLLEGE SPORTS SERIES

1. Schooling the Quarterback: (An M/M Tutor/Athlete Football Romance) ***

2. Testing the Goalie: (An M/M Professor/Student Hockey Romance) ***

3. Teasing the Winger: (An M/M Annoyances to Lovers Soccer Romance)

HUNTER SECURITY SERIES

1. Nixon: (An m/m bodyguard romance) ***

2. Denver: (An m/m best friends to lovers, single dad, bodyguard romance) ***

3. Knox: (A Suspenseful M/M Brother's Best Friend Romance) ***

4. Bennett: (An m/m bodyguard romance) ***

SULTRY SUMMER SERIES

1. Summer Heat (A FREE small town romance short story)

2. Long Summer Nights (A Small town low angst romance)

3. Summer Daze (A Small Town Interracial romance)

4. Summer Memories (A M/M second chance small town romance)***

5. Summer Dreams (A M/M Age Gap romance)***

LOVE IN SIENNA SERIES

1. Secret Smiles (A friends to lovers rock star romance) *ALSO AVAILABLE IN AUDIO!*

2. Hidden Kisses (An enemies to lovers baseball romance)

3. Guarded Hearts (A New adult, best friends to lovers, single mother romance.

4. Whispered Desires (A single mother, enemies to lovers, age gap, rock star romance)

5. Confidential Moments (A M/M Baseball romance)***

6. Clean Slates (A fast burn rock star romance)

7. Tangled Love (A rock star romance love triangle romance)

8. Restless Beat (A rock star romance)

9. Love In Sienna Boxset (Books 1-4)

10. Love in Sienna Boxset (Books 5-8)

SENTINEL PROTECTION DUOLOGY

1. Fighting Attraction (A M/M bodyguard romance)***

2. Embracing Temptation (A M/M age gap bodyguard romance)***

STANDALONES

Monster In The Shadows (Dark romance standalone)

Kissing in the snow (A M/M Christmas Novella set in the Sentinel Protection World)***

Afterglow (A kinky brother's best friend romance)

ACKNOWLEDGMENTS

Thank you so much for reading Testing the Goalie.I truly hope you loved reading it!

Now onto the thank you's. There are always so many people to thank and I really hope I don't miss anyone. (But if I do I'm sorry.)

First, I want to thank my amazing team. They are the real MVPs and they are always there when I need them. Honestly I don't know how I'd do it without them. I probably would just quit if it wasn't for there support. They are more than just PA's they are my friends and I value them more than words could say. So give it up for the women I couldn't live without, Brittany Franks and Suzanne Talkington!

Secondly, I want to thank my superb Alpha/Beta Readers Mandy, Robin, and Shannon. These ladies are always pointing out the beginning issues and are always available for me to bounce ideas off of. I'd probably still be stuck trying to figure things out if it wasn't for them.

Next, my sensitivity reader for making sure that Ian and Ben were portrayed properly. J.P Jaxson is an amazing human being that I am so lucky to call a friend and makes sure that I never miss represent the gay community. I love that he calls me out when needed and holds me to a high standard, I wouldn't want anything less.

My AMAZING editing team who helped me polish this book and make it as strong as it is today! Chantell, Lisa, Nikki, and Kaylene at Swish Designs and Editing were so amazing to work with and I don't think I am ever going to let them go.

My cover far too talented designer (who I already mentioned earlier but who also definitely deserves a second mention) Brittany Franks! Brittany is a one of a kind person and I am beyond lucky to have found her and claim her as one of my friends. She is simply the best person in the entire world. Not only is she immensely talented but she's also genuinely the most caring person I have ever met. I truly love this woman with all my heart and am NEVER letting her go.

My family for putting up with me when I put myself on a deadline and go a little crazy.

And last but obviously not least... you... the reader... without you I wouldn't be continuing to put books out! Thank you for your continued support. I love you all so much!

ABOUT THE AUTHOR

Laura is a steamy romance author from Alberta, Canada, who melds love and angst together while normalizing mental illness. She also brings a mixture of m/m and m/f books because love is love. In her books, you will fall in love with her rock stars, bodyguards, baseball players, a small town, a 2SLGBTQIA+ friendly University, and even a hired hit man!

When she's not writing, Laura enjoys reading, going to concerts, hiking, and experimenting with makeup!